THE VANISHING SMUGGLER

The firelight danced mockingly on the faces of
the three men

The
Vanishing Smuggler

BY
STEPHEN CHALMERS

ILLUSTRATIONS BY NESBITT BENSON

WILDSIDE PRESS

CONTENTS

LIST OF ILLUSTRATIONS

THE VANISHING SMUGGLER

CHAPTER I

THE GENESIS OF "SMUGGLE-ERIE"

THE winter moon, glowing like a tearful eye through the fog, revealed only a few of the scattered houses that stood for the Scotch village of Morag. In the dense mist the walls rose in the hoar-silvered light like circular piles of Druidic ruins.

The great estuary of the Clyde lay like dull metal under the moon halo, and the ripples sucked under a fringing of ice, for so intense was the frost that the Arctic finger encroached upon the salt sea.

It was midnight, yet the hour seemed full of whisperings. The bellowing of the foghorn on the Renfrewshire coast opposite, and the melancholy clang of the Gantock bell on the midreef, sounded a strange presage of evil.

In the coast-guard station, on the barren rocks at the north end of Morag Bay, old Jack Cookson turned uneasily on his bed. Every now and then he got up, pulled aside the curtain of the little window overlooking the bay, and peered through the moonlit fog. Once he grunted decisively; put on his big, blue reefer coat; jammed his sugarloaf hat on his head; stuck an ancient telescope under the flipper of the arm that was shot off at Trafalgar, and stamped away into the night, with a great snorting and blowing. But although he paraded the whole sweep of the bay, he noted neither sight nor sound that aroused his suspicion.

So the coast-guard went back to the station; carefully wiped the hoar off the venerable telescope; hung it on a rack by the side of his bunk, and presently, with many a snort, he resumed his uneasy slumbers.

He was not the only restless sleeper that night. In the garret of Giles Scrymegeour's house in the center of the village, there was a little fellow with a toothache. He was eight years of age.

This was in the year 1815, but there was something about that toothache which caused him to remember it through many a later year. As he lay on his bed of old meal-bags—for Giles Scrymegeour, his guardian, was a mean man—he somehow associated the foghorn and the Gantock bell and the smell of the meal-bags with his own misery.

He did not cry. Little Dick Scrymegeour was not of that sort. His experience was that crying profited nothing. He never got anything when he cried—anything he wanted. Old Giles would scold him and send him to his garret, with a half-slice of dry bread and a "tinny" of water, after repeating for the thousandth time how he had taken the lad out of the poorhouse, where they got skilly and water and dry bread, even on feast-days.

Little Dick did not remember his poorhouse days, nor his parents, whom the miser had ruined in some way or other; but sometimes, when he was not too hungry, he would take his "tinny" of water and bit of bread, and go sullenly to his garret. Once there, he would bar the door, and feed the bread to the mice, the while swearing in his little pagan heart that when he was strong enough he would take Giles Scryme-geour—Old Scryme, they called him—and slowly and deliberately strangle him with his hands.

Whing! went a shaft of toothache through his face as he rehearsed how he would commit the murder. He opened his eyes and looked up at the slanting roof of the garret, as one will do in the night of pain. The dark seemed full of red spots and fiery tadpoles. *Whing!* A groan fairly burst from the little stoic's lips. He rose and felt in the dark for his kilt, for he slept in his only other garment. He dressed in the dark, Giles having taken away the candle. The boy had made up his mind to go and wake up the dominie, a kind old man—the father of the village—

[3]

doctor, dentist, magistrate, and scholar—and ask him to pull the tooth. It was quite a brave thing for a lad of eight to contemplate, but—*whing!*—little Dick had learned independence of action in the bitter school of an orphan's experience.

When he was fully dressed, except for his shoes—if they can be called garments—he took these in his left hand, quietly undid the latch, and crept down the rickety wooden stairs to the back door. One of these days, the waif reflected, he would prowl downstairs just like this, when he went to murder old Giles. But that time was not yet.

He had just opened the back door when he stopped with a great thump of his heart. Something was wrong here. The door had not even been on the latch—a thing quite incredible in the house of the miser, Giles Scrymegeour. Filled with the sudden fear of a specter at his elbow, the boy slowly turned his head. There was nothing there but another door, which led into Giles's shop. Here the miser kept his stock of cheeses and cloths, and the old iron box which was said to be full of deeds and mortgages and similar weapons for wringing the hearts and pockets of his neighbors.

What stirred the boy to wild curiosity was a ray of candle-light, shining through the keyhole; and also he heard voices on the other side of the shop door. His guardian—Uncle Giles, as he was taught

to call him—should, by all custom, be asleep at this
hour; and, even if Dick had not heard the voices,
he was sure that Old Scryme would never waste a
candle in this fashion. He would rather sit in the
dark.

In another moment the eye of the little pagan
was at the keyhole, and in the same instant his toothache was gone—quite gone. In after years the mere
memory of that night was enough to cure him of
the worst toothache. On the iron box—this is what
he saw!—was a lighted candle stuck in an empty
bottle. The glow from the flame fell upon a pile of
golden guineas, and lit up the claw hands of his
Uncle Giles as he counted the money into several
smaller piles. And the same glow cast queer shadows
on the faces of several rough sailormen, who stood
round the box and the candle and the gold, and
glared down upon every movement of the miser's
claw hands with suspicion and avarice.

One of the group, a great, bearded, broad-shoul-
dered giant, whose face was of nobler cast than the
others, suddenly stuck out his long arms and, like
a watchman forcing a crowd with a staff, pushed the
men back with a growl.

The little eavesdropper's ear relieved his eye at
the keyhole.

"—like a pack of carrion crows," he heard the big
man say. " Ye'll get your deserts by and by.

Dinna be in a hurry. Better men than you have got more than they bargained for by being in ower great a hurry."

The others obeyed him as if he were the acknowledged master. And this was what set the boy at the keyhole thinking. He knew the man. There was none in Morag but would have known him—a pillar of the kirk—a leading man of the burgh. What was he doing here, in the company of three others whose names were a byword for poaching and smuggling? Most of all, what was he doing at dead of night in the disreputable shop of Giles Scrymegeour, the miser, a man whom this same pillar of respectability had more than once denounced as a public menace? And counting golden guineas? The little pagan glued his ear to the keyhole.

" Sixty-four guineas an' not a bawbee less!" one of the men was saying.

" But the risk's mine!" whined Old Scryme. " Think o't, man, and, forbye, I havena seen the stuff."

" Risk!" snapped the bearded giant. " Who speaks o' risk? Take it, or leave it, Giles Scrymegeour. My work's done. The stuff is where you know how to dispose of it. Enough of this gabbling. *Pay!* "

The leader rapped his knuckles on the box in a

[6]

way that sent Old Scryme's claws to rattling the guineas like metal castanets.

The boy's heart beat wildly. He crouched on his knees, leaning his face against the door, loath to miss a word.

Strangely and evilly informed for his years, he knew what was going on before him. So Uncle Giles was a smuggler—worse than a smuggler—the man who played the fiddle when the smugglers danced! The boy's soul soared with delight. He had a vision of his guardian's face next time he offered him dry bread and water for supper. He would ask him when he expected another midnight visit from Heather Bloom, the notorious smuggler!

But to think that Heather Bloom was—why, it was incredible! It had been whispered of the others; in fact, there was hardly a full-grown man in Morag who could plead not guilty to a charge of smuggling; but to think that Heather Bloom—fearless Heather Bloom—whom old Jack Cookson and Collector Horneycraft would have sold their honor to identify, was none other than——

The boy's legs, cramped up under him on the floor, suddenly slid outward and he crashed against the door. At the same moment the light in the keyhole went out and there came a sudden jangle of money, then a momentary silence, broken at length by a fear-stricken whisper inside the room:

"Did ye hear't? Guid forgie us, there's a revenue spy ahint the door!"

"Quiet!" came a tense whisper. "If that man escapes, we're all in jail."

The boy on the other side of the door had been petrified with fright for a moment, but at the first whispering his wits returned. He silently picked up his shoes and crept to the back door, which was still open to the misty moonlight.

Then, with a yell of excitement and defiance, he darted away, heedless of the sharp, icy stones that stabbed the soles of his feet. The moment the yell sounded, the smugglers, all except Giles Scrymegeour, —who crammed the gold into the iron box and then sat down, wringing his hands and whining,—dashed out of the miser's house and after the retreating figure, which loomed large and manlike in the fog. Once the leader of the smugglers stopped, put his fingers to his mouth, and whistled in a peculiar way. Then the chase began in silent earnest.

The fog was thicker than ever, and to the lad's imagination the horn-bellowing seemed louder and the Gantock bell-clang more menacing. He could hardly see ten yards before him, but he knew every stick and stone in Morag, and within five miles of it. Otherwise he would have been overtaken, or trapped, before he had gone two hundred yards; for he presently became aware that he was being pursued, not only by the four smugglers he had seen in Uncle Giles's shop, but by others who began to appear mysteriously from different directions.

The blood coursed in his veins faster and hotter. In spite of his physical fear, this was a game he liked and of which, in the child-play sense, he was a master. It was the great and glorious game of " smuggle-erie," and among the children of Morag this same lad Dick was known as " Smuggle-erie." Swift of foot, alert of eye, and cunning of mind, there was not a hiding-place in the village that he did not know, and there was many a refuge of which the other boys did not dream, when little Dick was the " smuggler " to be caught.

As he ran, he laughed to think how he could outwit these clumsy-footed grown-ups. Several times voices behind him cried to voices in the fog before him, and thrice he narrowly escaped plunging into the arms of a figure that would suddenly loom out of the mist; but ever the supple ankle and swift foot carried him like a deer from danger.

Once, when they had closed in all around him, he stood perfectly still. Two smugglers ran out and grappled with one another in the fog. He dashed past them and, slipping behind a rock, yelled at the top of his lungs that glorious whoop of the game:

" *Smuggle-erie!* "

[9]

The Vanishing Smuggler

But that was the only sound. The old coast-guard may have heard it, or only thought he heard it, and turned over to dream once more of the battle of Trafalgar. The smugglers themselves pursued their quarry with never a sound, save a quiet call or a whistle and, once, a sharp curse of alarm when the boy shouted the guilty word.

Aye! it was a game of smuggle-erie—the *real* game; and Dick Scrymegeour reveled in it. He was no longer afraid of the smugglers. They were playfellows, to his boy mind. He had never a thought of physical violence now. It was his cunning against theirs in the game of all games that he loved the most.

But in a little while his breath came quick and short; there was a sharp, continuous pain in his side. Smuggle-erie was glad when he found a hiding-place where he could remain in safety for a few minutes, and he grew chary of uttering the cry that kept the pot boiling and told his enemies of his whereabouts. But the smugglers were relentless. The safety of every man of them hung by the capture of that eavesdropper, who darted hither and thither with a shout which, to their understanding, meant only a warning to the coast-guard. The smugglers spread like game-beaters, and advanced in a broadside line, stealthily peering into the doorways of the cottages, behind rocks and under the overturned boats on the

beach. Morag slept through it all, or, if awake,
it was peculiarly deaf.

The chase had been in full cry for fifteen minutes
when Smuggle-erie cast around in his mind for a
supreme trick that would end the game and allow
him a clear course to the back door of Giles Scrymegeour's house. Between him and his garret was the
line of smugglers, and by this time he had been
forced almost to the south end of the village. Beyond there was nothing but the bleak, frozen hills—
a dire place for a night's lodging—and the fir woods
surrounding the laird's castle.

Then a refuge occurred to the boy's mind—a
hiding-place, the very nature of which sent a chill
through his blood. A few hundred yards beyond
the southern extremity of the village, and by the gate
entering the laird's estate, was an old gardener's
lodge, which had stood tenantless for as long as
Smuggle-erie could remember. The place was re-
puted a haunt of ghosts.

Smuggle-erie was running toward this sinister
place before he fully realized what chances he was
taking with the supernatural. Once a great black
bull had swum in from the sea to the Bull Rock,
a headland fronting the lodge on the sea side, and
had drowned because it could not scramble up the
slippery sides of the massive bowlder. Ever since
then, legend had a picturesque description of a gigan-

tic black bull, which was to be seen o' nights round
the rock and the lodge and the fir plantation, charg-
ing about with fiery eyes and flaming nostrils.

Many a time the unkempt ward of the miser had
challenged his boy companions to visit the lodge by
night, but, somehow, the daring had never become
a deed. Now, Smuggle-erie was about to make a
virtue of a necessity, but, as he strove to assure
himself, he had never believed in ghosts, anyway.

He had little time in which to choose, at the best
of it. His sole chance of winning the game of
smuggle-erie lay in reaching that haunted lodge.
He never supposed for a moment that any of his
pursuers would enter the place—so great, indeed, was
the local terror of the black bull. But they were
close behind him. They had run straight upon his
heels from the last point where he emerged to view.

Again the peculiar whistle sounded. It sent an
uneasy pang through the boy's heart, but it was too
late now to choose any other course. His feet were
bruised and half frozen by the stones, and the thumb
and finger which gripped his shoes were painfully
cramped. By the time he reached the lodge, he
was too glad to have arrived to care anything about
ghosts. But no sooner had he sprung into the
haunted place than his heart gave a great leap, then
stopped as if frozen.

He could see nothing but a dazzling glare of light,

as he came to an astonished halt in the middle of the damp, rotten floor.

For a moment he thought he had come face to face with the bull, but as his eyes became used to the glare, he discovered that it came from a lamp in the hand of a man; and there were a dozen other men in the place, besides a fine array of bales, barrels, and miscellaneous merchandise, piled on the floor.

" Hey! " ejaculated the man who held the lamp. " What's this? "

The man was too astonished to lay hands upon Smuggle-erie, even. The lad stood there, blinking and panting and grinning, and wondering why they all looked so startled— so frightened! Then the night was filled with a rushing of feet. Next moment Heather Bloom and half a dozen men dashed into the lodge and slammed the door tight after them.

" Have ye got him? " Heather Bloom asked sharply.

" N-na! " stammered the man with the lamp. " But there's a lad—Scrymegeour's lad—tumbled in here like a shot."

Then there was silence. Heather Bloom, at first amazed, then suspicious, then with a slow-dawning sense of the ridiculous, gazed upon the boy who had put the fear of death into the hearts of a score of smugglers. And Smuggle-erie, himself, gazed upon his captors with a defiant, triumphant smile. Boy though he was, he knew now that it was a serious game he had been playing, for there were men here— in league with smugglers, if not smugglers themselves —whose revealed identity would have set the country- side by the ears. And there was the stuff on the floor, although how it could have got to this place was beyond Smuggle-erie's understanding. He was in possession of a secret—a secret which had been guarded in Morag with the honor of every individual family in it. The boy broke the silence with an embarrassed gulp.

" I beat ye! " he chuckled.

There was no answer to that. Heather Bloom and his men stood there in amazed, puzzled silence. What was to be done with the lad? The chief of the smugglers nodded his head up and down, like a man who is confronted by an unpleasant fact. Then there came a scratching and whining at the door.

" Let me in! " pleaded a voice. " For Guid's sake, let me in. The coast-gaird's right at my heels! "

Heather Bloom spun around, pulled the door open, and dragged Giles Scrymegeour into the light.

" And if the coast-guard *was* at your heels," he snarled, " ye'd still show them the way, wouldn't ye? Now, look ye here. This is your lad, is it not? What's to be done with him? "

"Lad, how would you like to be a real smuggler?"

Page 15

The Genesis of " Smuggle-erie "

The boy lifted his eyes and fixed them savagely upon his guardian's face. There was something in them that made Old Scryme turn pale.

" Was't him? " he whispered.

" Aye—him! " said Heather Bloom. " What's to be done with the lad? He kens enough to wring your neck, Master Giles Scrymegeour."

The miser's face screwed up into evil wrinkles, and his eyes danced furtively. He suddenly turned to the men and spoke as if to excuse his suggestion.

" If he goes back to Morag, there's no one o' us 'll be oot o' jail in a week! " he cried. " It's a desp'rit sittyation—a desp'rit sittyation! "

" Maybe," said the leader quietly, " ye would have no objection, Giles, if we tied a stone to the brat's feet and dropped him ower the Bull Rock? "

" It might be for the best," muttered the miser, turning up the whites of his eyes. " It's a very desp'rit sittyation! "

Heather Bloom threw his hands in the air with an expression of disgust.

" Grogblossom," he said to a smuggler with a fat, pig-like face, " take this lad aboard the schooner and, as ye value your neck, keep him safe. " Lad, he added, turning to the boy, " how would ye like to be a *real* smuggler? "

And the boy, boy-like, replied:

" Fine, sir!"

" Very well," said Heather Bloom. With a contemptuous glance at Giles Scrymegeour, he added: " It's a blessing for us and a pity for the lad that there's none to say no to it."

CHAPTER II

TWELVE years later the little signal cannon in the Thistle Down's bows boomed through the late dusk, and the schooner's anchor splashed merrily into the waters of Morag Bay.

"Well, well!" cried Grogblossom, the fat cook, wiping his red, pig face as he stepped out of the galley. "Here we are, lads, an' bless't if the auld toon's no in the same place. Noo, Red Heid," he added, waddling toward a short fiery-haired man who leaned by the gunwale, "will ye promise to get yer hair cut afore we put to sea ag'in?"

"Lemme hair alone!" growled the Red Mole. "It's nae worse than your face."

"Hoot, toot!" protested Grogblossom. "It's the galley fire, man—the galley fire. Well, well! An' there's auld Morag, as fine a sight for sore eyes as ye'd want after a' they French frog-stools. It's a sayin', ye ken, that a' things change, but the Bible must ha' meant everything excep' Morag. Losh, man, I'll swear there's no been a hoose built in my time."

[17]

The Red Mole turned away and looked impatiently up and down the deck. He seemed assured, presently, by the calm poise of Captain Grant, as the commander stood by the wheel and waved a hand to someone in an approaching boat.

"The whole pack o' them 'll be aboard in a minute," said the Red Mole to Grogblossom. "Man, I've been through this thing a score o' times, an' I'm still fear't."

"Hoot, toot!" said Grogblossom. "Ye'd think a man wi' a heid like yours would no be afeared o' anything. But I was thinkin' there's been changes in Morag, after a'. There's a few mair bairns an' a few mair graves in the kirkyard. An'—there comes the lass, Red Mole! See her comin' off in the boat yonder wi' the dominie. Hech, sir! I mind the night her mother dee'd—same night we brung Smuggle-erie aboard. Puir Mistress Grant! Aye, aye. Change an' decay—change an' decay, even in Morag!"

"It's him I'm feared o'," growled the Red Mole; "aye, ever since that very night."

"Who?" asked the cook, waking up from his mournful thoughts.

"The skipper," was the reply. "It's my opeenion he'll take to releegion afore long, he's that fu' o' auld wives' warnin's. It makes an or'nar' man nervous. He's goin' doon the hill, Grogblossom—

[18]

doon the hill. If it was no for Smuggle-erie, there'd never be a drop run through."

" Doon the hill—aye, aye! " sighed Grogblossom. " No wunner. The man's got a conscience, like mysel'. It was his evil transgressions that sent her gray hairs in sorrer to the grave."

" She hadna gray hairs," protested the Red Mole stolidly.

" Na? " murmured Grogblossom. " Maybe she had a red heid. Well, here's the rev'nue boat. I'm off! An' here's luck to Smuggle-erie! " He waddled back into the galley, but gave the Red Mole a shock by turning and saying deliberately: " I wunner if it's true that a body's hair grows in the coffin after——"

" Shut up! " growled the Red Mole, turning away, much perturbed.

Captain Grant, in the meantime, stood awaiting the revenue boat, which shot out from the coast-guard station with old Jack Cookson aboard; also Mr. Horneycraft, collector of revenue, and Lieutenant Ben Larkin, a young naval officer recently appointed to the coast-guard service in a determined effort to suppress smuggling. The nefarious trade had been growing to an alarming extent along the west coast of Scotland, and particularly in the vicinity of Morag.

Indeed, the daring with which contraband was

being trafficked in the Firth of Clyde had at last
aroused the special attention of the government.
The famous Heather Bloom, a personage whose existence had been more or less doubted for fifteen years,
partly because it was impossible to place his identity,
had convinced the revenue authorities by his daring
exploits that he was no myth, and that his was the
clever brain which directed the successful smuggling
of recent years. When young Ben Larkin got his
commission from the Lords of the Admiralty, he received a clap on the back from a friendly well-wisher
and the hint that if he captured the man, or even
discovered his identity, there would be greater honor
in store for him.

It was in pursuance of his rigid policy of thoroughly examining the credentials of every vessel that
moved in or near Morag waters, that Lieutenant
Larkin accompanied the coast-guard and Mr. Horneycraft aboard the Thistle Down. Not that he or
his associates expected to discover anything suspicious or contraband about the schooner, which was
a Morag-owned, Morag-manned craft, plying with
oats, broadcloth, and general merchandise between
the Scotch village and English ports; but the clever-
ness of Heather Bloom demanded that every pre-
caution be taken.

In this instance there might well have been excuse
for special attention to the Thistle Down, for the

schooner had just returned after one of her very rare trips to Bordeaux, and vessels out of that French port were ever worthy of close inspection. As Mr. Horneycraft put it, in his misanthropic way of thinking and speaking:

" There are lads aboard and lasses ashore, and the French make fine gewgaws."

It was impossible to know Mr. Horneycraft for five minutes without discovering the principal peculiarity of his character. That strain of suspiciousness which is common to man and animal, was developed in him to an abnormal degree. It may have been born in him, or engendered by the nature of his profession, but it is certain that he believed all men were malefactors, if not in deed, at least by inclination. As old Jack Cookson would say of him:

" Mr. Horneycraft, sir, would look for contraband under the chair you offered him, by thunder! "

Of this old sea-dog, what he could not say for himself was never worth saying about him. He had fought under Nelson at Trafalgar, sir, and was a loyal subject of King George, bless 'im! and he had a set of principles from which no man could force him to depart, by thunder! It was he who relieved a certain stiffness when the three occupants of the revenue boat boarded the Thistle Down and were greeted by Captain John Grant.

" I notice," said Mr. Horneycraft icily, " that

your vessel invariably arrives unexpectedly, Captain Grant."

" For you, possibly," retorted the skipper, with the ghost of a hard smile.

" And always at dawn, or late dusk," said Mr. Horneycraft.

" By the sailor's timepiece, it's all one," said the captain.

" Spoken like a British sailor!" cried the coastguard, sticking out his one and only hand to Captain Grant, who gripped it with a laugh. " Why, sir," said old Cookson, " my old Admiral, Horatio Nelson, waited for neither dark nor daylight. 'There's the enemy!' ses 'e. 'Let 'er go, my lads! Westminster Abbey or victory!' And before midnight, by thunder, we blew the French flagship sky-high! Yes, sir—*sky-high!* "

" Well, gentlemen," said the captain, " I want to get ashore. Will you step into the cuddy? The papers are all ready."

Lieutenant Ben Larkin had been running his eyes over the vessel and her commander, while old Jack Cookson was breaking the icicles between Horneycraft and Grant. It was a favorite suspicion of Horneycraft's that the Thistle Down was a sailing hotbed of contraband. She was the only vessel of any size which sailed in and out of Morag Bay. Her owner was her commander, Grant, although it

The Thistle Down Comes to Port

was said that Richard Halliday, the laird, had an interest in her, and rumor had it also that old Giles Scrymegeour, too, had his talons in the pie.

Giles, it may be worth noting, controlled most of the business in Morag, which was the trade center of a large part of the district known as Cowal. Even the capital of Argyll, Inveraray, drew a large amount of her supplies through Morag, which was conveniently situated on the Clyde and within easy reach of Glasgow. It has ever been a matter for surprise that Morag has not grown in size and commercial importance, but even to this day the duke has refused franchise to that main artery of industry, the railway.

The Thistle Down was a craft of some seventy tons burden, and presented a more graceful yacht-like appearance than was usual in Clyde craft of her size. Lieutenant Ben Larkin saw with a sailor's eye that she was a sleek, slippery vessel, and her white decks and shimmering brass-work spoke of a discipline quite in accordance with the appearance of her master, Captain Grant. The skipper was a tall, broad-beamed man, heavy-browed and bearded. He spoke little and led the way to the schooner's cuddy with a decisiveness that was equal to a command to follow. While Horneycraft's suspicious eye peered at the ship's papers the master stood by, respectful and attentive, but with a hint of defiance in the way he leaned his hand on the table, the fist shut, and a faint smile hovering about his brown beard.

"Quite satisfactory," said Mr. Horneycraft, and added, almost like an afterthought, "Of course!"

"Thank you," said the captain.

"You must pardon me, Captain Grant," Mr. Horneycraft went on, "but with your permission, Mr. Cookson and I will look over the ship."

"The permission is unnecessary," replied Grant ironically.

"Merely a form," put in the lieutenant, half ashamed of Mr. Horneycraft's lack of tact. "This Heather Bloom, you know——"

"Yes?" said the captain, his face like a steel trap.

"This Heather Bloom is giving a lot of trouble. In my business, you know," and Larkin laughed lightly, "a man is not permitted to trust his own brother. I am sure Mr. Horneycraft will make his visit as brief as possible."

"For that matter," said Captain Grant, with his cryptic smile, "he is welcome to remain aboard as long as he pleases. Grogblossom!" he added, raising his voice.

As the fat sailor with the moribund thoughts entered, the master waved a hand. It was like a preconcerted signal, for in another moment, Grogblossom, like a ponderous geni in a ludicrous Arabian tale, appeared with a tray, a bottle, and four glasses.

"To your good health, gentlemen!" said the captain, when the glasses were filled, and lifting his own with a gesture full of quiet dignity.

"Here's to Heather Bloom!" said Lieutenant Larkin jocularly.

"—when I catch him," added Mr. Horneycraft sourly.

"Here's to King George—bless 'im!" bellowed the old coast-guard, indignant at the omission, "and confound his enemies."

The glasses were raised with a laugh which heightened as the lieutenant cried, "and to the lady in the doorway."

Standing on the companion-steps and looking down into the cuddy, was the sweetest, freshest Scotch lass it had ever been the young officer's good luck to see.

"I looks toward you, madam," he called gallantly. And he could have sworn that she was sweeter than any lass of Richmond Hill when she courtesied, and laughingly gave the correct response to that old toast:

"'I observes it, sir, and likewise bows!'"

At the voice, Captain Grant set down his glass with a sudden ejaculation of pleasure.

"Ha! Grizel! I thought I saw you in the boat. And who was with you?"

"The dear old dominie," she cried exuberantly, "and Mr. Scrymegeour." It was interesting to note the shift of her expression from sunshine to shadow as she spoke the two names.

"And where's the dominie?" the captain asked.

"Coming! Coming!" said a voice from the companion. "Old bones, my friend, old bones. Crabbed age and youth, one might say, cannot walk together."

The figure of a fine old man, stooped with age, white-haired and with a long, thin beard of the same hue, came slowly down the companion, his thin hands clutching firmly at his staff handle, over which a bit of white lace fell in old-fashioned grace from the sleeve-cuff.

The dominie was the grand old man of Morag. He knew the pedigree of every man, woman, and child in the parish, and, as the village Æsculapius, he was acquainted with the personal idiosyncrasies, pathological tendencies, and inherited strains of each family. To him were referred for arbitration all questions of lore, learning, and law; for besides being a scholar of no mean order in those times, he was a bailie in the land, and when the occasion arose administered a queer mixture of moral philosophy and legal justice.

Behind him as he came down the companion-steps

was Giles Scrymegeour, the miser. As both entered the cabin, the esteem in which either man was held was marked by the respectful enthusiasm with which the dominie was greeted, even by Horneycraft, and the manner in which Old Scryme, of equal years, slid like a rat into a corner, after grinning and nodding at each in turn.

"Well, business is business," said Old Scryme, when the usual welcomes to the ship were over.

At that, Mr. Horneycraft, having glanced at the label on the bottle which Grogblossom had set on the table, rose and prepared to go on a search through the ship.

But the voice of the girl stopped him. Grizel, after looking vainly around the cabin and expectantly eying the companion until her patience was exhausted, suddenly blurted out:

"Where's Smuggle-erie?"

The words were no sooner out of her mouth than Old Scryme, who had been running his nose over the lines of the manifest, gave a jump that brought all eyes upon him. The miser was trembling like a sick man. But Captain Grant looked up calmly, drew his hand over his daughter's brown hair, and said:

"Is he not aboard, lass? Then he must ha' gone ashore. I mind he had a bit of Valenciennes lace for you."

[27]

" Indeed," said Horneycraft, his tone full of triumph, and his eyes flashing from the cringing Old Scryme to Lieutenant Larkin. " Who gave anyone permission to leave this ship? "

The captain's eyes turned full upon him.

" You speak to me, I take it? "

" Aye, to you. You have been long enough master of a ship to be aware that no person may leave it before it has been cleared by his majesty's revenue officer? "

" I am aware of it," said Grant stonily.

" You are aware of it! " snapped the exasperated Mr. Horneycraft. " Yet you calmly inform me that one Smuggle-erie—— "

" Gentlemen! Gentlemen! " protested the dominie, while Lieutenant Larkin grew red and old Jack Cookson snorted loudly.

" —that Smuggle-erie—a likely name—leaves the ship with a piece of Valenciennes lace."

" I believe I said so to my girl, here," said Captain Grant, a red glow spreading around his temples. " Be careful what you say, now, Master Busybody."

" Spoken like an Englishman! " the coast-guard burst out.

" Busybody," sneered Mr. Horneycraft, his face livid with shock. " Be none too sure that my busyness has been in vain, Captain Grant, or that the master of the Thistle Down has not a name like his vessel——"

Captain Grant's fist came down on the table with a sharp but quiet impact. The air became charged with menace.

Horneycraft's words died in his throat as the lion-like sea-master rose to full length before him.

Grant's face was pale, but his eyes and his tongue were like lithe steel.

" King's officer or no," he said, " if you apply that name to me in the presence of my girl, I will lift you by the scruff of your scrawny neck and drop you overboard! "

CHAPTER III

THE captain's threat produced embarrassment upon all in the cabin of the Thistle Down. At a sign from her father, Grizel fled to the deck. The skipper, quietly but firmly, faced Mr. Horneycraft. The dominie and the coast-guard both protested, the former in gentle terms, the latter in a series of indignant snorts. In the corner was Giles Scrymegeour, a damp, quivering, despicable heap. The only man who acted with any degree of promptitude was the lieutenant, Ben Larkin.

" Mr. Horneycraft," he said sharply, " while it is my duty to support you in matters of this kind, I am surprised at the stand you have taken. No doubt, Captain Grant erred in permitting any of his crew to leave the ship before you cleared her, but your insinuation with regard to a lad who has stolen off, eager to see his—his mother, perhaps, is absurd, based as it is upon a quibble."

With that, the lieutenant marched up the companion with a manly squaring of his shoulders. The coast-guard followed with an explosive " Spoken like an Englishman!" The dominie sorrowfully tailed after, wagging his thin, white beard in elderly disapprobation.

Left alone with the big-jawed skipper—for the existence of Giles Scrymegeour was overlooked— Horneycraft suddenly weakened and bolted.

The moment he was gone, Captain Grant swooped down upon Old Scryme.

"Listen to me, Master Scrymegeour," said he, with wrath and scorn. "I've been sick of you for twenty years. Now, I'm sick of your service. I want you to understand from this minute that the Thistle Down has cheated the customs for the last time. And that's my last word. You can take your own time to swallow it."

And he, too, marched out of the cabin. Giles Scrymegeour sat for a full minute, wet and pallid with fright. It was easy to see that the man's heart was constitutionally weak. But in a moment his terror passed and his breath, which had been blowing through wide-parted bluish lips, began to draw through his teeth. Into his eyes, too, came the accustomed sheen of cunning.

"We'll see! We'll see!" he said, half aloud.

Then he gathered up the papers, stuffed them in his pockets, and scurried up the stairs, for all the world like a rat on a still-hunt.

Lieutenant Ben Larkin, in the meantime, had forgotten his wrath the moment he reached the deck. The Thistle Down now presented an animated scene. Although it was almost dark, the Morag folk had taken advantage of the coming of the ship and the fine autumn evening, to make a gala-night of it. Lads and lasses and village worthies were swarming aboard to welcome sons and lovers from foreign shores, for in those days it was a far cry to France, and especially to Bordeaux, which entailed the voyage through the dreaded Bay of Biscay and up the stream of the Garonne. And the foreign wonders which the sailors brought to sleepy little Morag after such a trip, aroused an excitement which was not equaled even by the annual Highland games at Inveraray.

But, although the picture charmed Lieutenant Larkin—the lasses in their Sunday finery and the sailors with their white socks and knotted kerchiefs— the thing that most pleased his eye was the girl he had seen in the cabin.

Grizel was about seventeen years old, still girlish, but carrying herself with the modesty and inexplicable grace of dawning womanhood. She was the nut-brown lass of song, with her glossy hair, honest, full, brown eyes, soft sun-tanned skin and white teeth which, Ben swore to himself, were like coral reefs and as dangerous to a sailor. She cut a pretty figure in her short skirt, big-bowed shoes, bright-buttoned, sleeveless jacket and Tam-o'-Shanter, as she kept step with strutting old Jack Cookson on the poop-deck.

The coast-guard, of course, was monopolizing the conversation, and anyone could have judged the topic by the angle of the telescope under the arm-stump and the way he pointed heroically to the upper rigging of the schooner. One expected to see the picture rounded off with a ball from the crow's-nest of the Redoubtable and Nelson falling upon the quarter-deck of the Thistle Down.

Larkin was waiting his chance to capture the pretty lass, while pretending to be looking over the ship's side, where a dozen rowboats crowded around the revenue cutter, which was neatly manned by bluejackets. A hand suddenly fell upon the lieutenant's arm—the stealthy, impressive, important hand of Mr. Horneycraft. The collector's face was still pale with anger, and when he spoke it was in a spiteful undertone, full of omen for the subject.

" I thank you, lieutenant, for your support in the unpleasant incident downstairs," he said, with quiet incision. " Nevertheless, I hope to impress upon you that your mole-hill is my mountain. If this person, Smuggle-erie——"

Larkin's brows knitted irritably.

" If this Smuggle-erie," Mr. Horneycraft persisted

calmly, " left the schooner, as it is admitted he did, how did he go?—swim? "

And Mr. Horneycraft, with a fine gesture of triumph, waved his hands round at the schooner's boats, which hung intact upon the davits.

At one glance Lieutenant Larkin knew that no boat belonging to the schooner had, as yet, been lowered. But he turned angrily upon Horneycraft.

" You are talking nonsense, sir! " he cried. " Are there not a dozen boats alongside, and——"

" He left in none of them! " retorted Mr. Horneycraft. " My inquiries have determined that. Besides, I took the liberty of instructing your bluejackets before——"

" Indeed," said the lieutenant, his face flushing. " Then I have no manner of doubt that the man did not leave the ship after we came aboard."

" Well? " sneered Mr. Horneycraft.

" Well! " the lieutenant fairly shouted. " I suppose, as you say, he swam ashore."

" Not necessarily," the revenue collector responded sweetly. " Perhaps a boat met the Thistle Down in the offing before she——"

The lieutenant smiled.

" Quite possible, Mr. Horneycraft," he interrupted; " but I fancy you are trying to make facts to fit your suspicions. Far be it from me——"

He stopped short and his eyes suddenly widened

with wonder. They had been conversing by the gunwale, amidships, and not three paces from the door of the cook's galley.

The lieutenant had suddenly turned to discover the moribund Grogblossom looking straight at himself and Horneycraft, and with an expression on his face that betokened considerable interest in what he was overhearing. But the moment his eyes met Larkin's, Grogblossom's face took on its usual pig look and he busied himself scouring a frying-pan, at the same time whistling a tune with unusual rapidity. It was the lively air of a quaint old Scotch song, and after he had run through a verse, Grogblossom began at the beginning again:

" Pease brose again, mither, pease brose again!"

Then an odd thing happened. From some other part of the ship, the air of the second line was smartly taken up:

" Ye feed me like a blackbird and me yer only wean!"

Grogblossom's whistle had stopped short to admit the second line, but as soon as it was finished, his fat lips pursed and he was off again with the third and fourth lines.

" That's queer!" thought Larkin.

He listened intently but, although Grogblossom

went on whistling shrilly, the clever interpolation did not recur, and presently the lieutenant was willing to admit that his ear had played him a trick.

When he turned away, Horneycraft had vanished, and at the same time Larkin saw the coast-guard leave the poop. In a minute the gallant lieutenant was at Grizel's side, apologizing for Mr. Horneycraft's unseemly behavior in the cabin.

"Oh, everybody kens Mr. Horneycraft!" she said, in her frank, laughing Scotch tongue.

"And was it about the battle of the Nile, or Trafalgar, that old Jack was holding forth?"

"Neither, Mr. Clever," said she. "He was telling me about the time when he was stationed at Jamaica—place they make rum, sir—waiting for the French, by thunder! and Nelson on the lookout with his telescope, sir!——" She broke off her mimicry with a peal of laughter.

"I knew he'd get Nelson in somewhere," said Larkin, who, nevertheless, had a great respect for the old sea-dog who had seen England's greatest hero carried to the cock-pit.

"Tell me, captain," said she. "How many——"

"Lieutenant," he corrected modestly.

"Well, you'll be an admiral some day," she said, by way of comfort. "But tell me, how many smugglers have you caught since you came to Morag?"

"Why, I have only been here a week," he protested.

"But ye havena answered my question," she persisted mischievously. "How many smugglers have ye caught?"

"None so far," he admitted. "But Mr. Horneycraft is sure we are going to catch plenty before long. In fact," he added with a chuckle, "he has quite made up his mind that this Smuggle-erie is the terrible Heather Bloom."

"Oh," she said, in alarm. "That's not so."

He tried to see her face in the dusk, but could not.

"It's only a nickname," she said earnestly. "You see, he had it when he was a little lad, and it's stuck to him. Smuggle-erie's a game."

"A great game, indeed," he observed. "Tell me, Miss Grizel, who is this Smuggle-erie?"

"Smuggle-erie?" she echoed, after a perceptible pause. If it had been lighter he would have seen her color deepen. "Why, he's—he's Smuggle-erie."

"I'm not much wiser."

"Well—Smuggle-erie," she stammered, and the queer name fell from her tongue with a quaint turn, "Smuggle-erie's a nephew, in a way, to that man Scrymegeour."

"Oh!" he breathed comprehendingly.

"But Smuggle-erie's not like him, ye ken," she

hastened to correct. " He's only a kind of nephew. Smuggle-erie's—he's—he's very different!"

" Oh!" said Larkin once more, and this time the comprehending breath had a tinge of disappointment in it.

There was a moment's silence, which was, somehow, awkward.

Ben Larkin looked out over the dim, calm Firth of Clyde. He did not need to be told who Smuggle-erie was, as related to Grizel Grant.

And he felt more lonely over the knowledge than he had done over anything since he came to sleepy Morag. He supposed it was one of those village matches—a girl allotted to marry a man whom she respected only because she had become used to the idea of looking upon him as her future husband. He was probably some rascally sailor, stupidly romantic, brutally healthy, and notoriously evil. It seemed a pity—a shame. This girl, Grizel, was worthy of a better fate. But, of course, she would marry the sailor and, in time, she would develop into the long-tongued, slovenly matron that was so characteristic of Morag.

Something interrupted Larkin's train of pessimism. It was a boat gliding in toward the southern end of the cove from the open firth. He looked at the craft for a moment. The shapeless mass of the hull did not impress him until he suddenly noticed the movement of her rowers and observed with a mental start that the craft glided as silently as a phantom.

"What's that?" he asked sharply, breaking the pause in a way that startled the girl.

"That?" she said stupidly, her eye following the line of his extended arm. "That's a boat."

"A boat—of course. What boat?"

"How should I know?" she retorted stiffly. "Most like it's a fisherman."

"A fisherman," he said, half to himself. "It's more like a smuggler. Why are the oars muffled?"

"Exactly!" said Mr. Horneycraft, coming up behind. "Possibly the lieutenant, having done his best to obstruct my business, will now attend to his own."

Larkin felt the blood rush to his face, but he had no answer ready, except that of action.

"Mr. Horneycraft," he said sternly, "send Jack Cookson ashore at once. His orders are to find this man, Smuggle-erie, if he is in Morag. If not——"

"Oh, no, no, no!" cried Grizel suddenly, as if she had been hurt. "You are wrong! You are wrong!"

"My duty, madam," he replied shortly. "Rest assured of him if he is where he ought to be."

With that he left her hurriedly and dropped into the cutter.

A moment later she heard his voice raised in sharp

command and then came the splash of six oars striking the water simultaneously. Something new in
her life—a dread of the indefinable, a sense of in-
comprehensible evil—surrounded her suddenly. The
penny whistle which Grogblossom was blowing, lust-
ily, to the tune of "Pease brose again, mither,"
seemed fraught with this mysterious terror.—She
leaned over the stern of the schooner and stared at
the dim shadow of the strange boat, and her fear
rose in her throat as the cutter shot out to the
rhythmic music of trained oars. She heard her
father's step behind her, and his voice bidding her
get ready for the shore, but her response was a half-
hysterical cry:

"Father! They say Smuggle-erie's in yon boat,
and it's a smuggler."

"Who said so?" Grant asked sharply.

"The lieutenant—Mr. Horneycraft."

"Keep quiet, child!" he said sternly. "This is
mere blethering. You and I are going ashore to the
little home for supper."

His hand rested on her shoulder, but he made no
move to lead her away. Indeed, he stood by her side
and, in silence, watched the revenue cutter sweep
toward the headland called the Bull Rock. That
seemed to be the point toward which the mysterious
boat was moving. The latter craft was coming
straight in from the firth, and as the Thistle Down

The Vanishing Smuggler

lay at anchor near the north end of the bay, the courses of the two boats, when joined, would form a right angle. The boat with the muffled oars had about a quarter of a mile to go. To intercept her the cutter had more than half a mile to cover, but allowing for the superior speed and manning of the latter, the result of the race provided interesting speculation.

Mr. Horneycraft was another spectator of the contest, but his eyes did not linger on it as much as upon the crew of the Thistle Down.

Grogblossom had laid aside his penny whistle. He and the Red Mole, with a few others, were loitering about the larboard side of the schooner, furtively watching the cutter and her quarry.

" Strange! " reflected Mr. Horneycraft gleefully. " Not a man in a hundred would have noticed that boat, and yet they are staring as if their lives depended upon the result." And he smiled the smile of self-satisfaction.

Another witness was Giles Scrymegeour. Behind the mizzenmast he stood, washing his hands in invisible water. Once or twice he essayed to walk the deck, but to his guilty imagination it seemed that the whole world was watching the race, whereas Mr. Horneycraft's estimate of those who could have observed the incident was, indeed, not far wrong. But to Giles Scrymegeour it was as if every eye was upon him to see how he enjoyed the suspense. He crept back into the shadow of the mast and stayed there until the end came.

But to none was the upshot fraught with such tragedy as to Grizel Grant and her father. Minutes passed and they were still standing on the poop, his hand on her shoulder and his breath drawing deep and strong. She noticed a growing pressure of his hand, but ascribed it to her own strange agitation. Straight as an arrow the cutter shot toward the Bull Rock, and to that same point glided the silent boat from the sea. Now they were nearing. But two hundred yards divided the rock from the revenue cutter, and less than one hundred from the craft with the muffled oars. The cutter dashed through the water; the strange boat's speed increased. Now the respective distances from the rock were seventy-five yards and forty yards; now fifty yards and thirty; now thirty yards and less than twenty; fifteen yards and—the mysterious craft shot toward the haven in a last effort to evade the cutter.

Grizel's hand gripped her father's arm and a cry choked her. The skipper's breathing came to her ears in quick, heavy spasms. His hand gripped and tightened on her shoulder.

Between the cutter and the Bull Rock stood ten yards.

Even on the Thistle Down those who were watch-

ing could hear the voice of the lieutenant crying:
" Now, my lads! "

A few more strokes and the strange boat would
be intercepted. In any event she must be captured
before her bows grated on the beach, if indeed, there
was any beach within a hundred yards of that great
sea-bowlder.

A groan burst from her father's lips.

Grizel saw the boats seemingly merged together
for a moment in the angle of meeting; then——

" Thank God! " said Captain Grant, in a tense
whisper.

Grizel could hardly believe her eyes. The mysterious craft had suddenly vanished as if engulfed
in the sea or in the great rock. At the same moment
a command sounded over the darkling bay and the
revenue cutter was seen to run on her own impetus
with her oars trailing idly in the water.

" Gone! " Grizel cried in amazement.

In the stern of the cutter Lieutenant Ben Larkin
sat stupefied.

" Gone! " he gasped. Then awaking, like a man
who realizes that he has been the victim of some
optical illusion, he cried sharply to his men: " Which
way? "

" Beggin' your pardon, sir," said the bowman, all
in a shake. " That waren't no real boat, sir, beggin'
your pardon, sir."

The Vanishing Smuggler

"What rubbish is this!" thundered Larkin. "Are you all blind?" Then, becoming aware that he was losing his temper, he suddenly altered his tone. "Something wrong here, men! Come, there must be a passage."

At his command the cutter moved slowly into the shadow of the great black rock, which arose straight and slippery from the sea. Behind it, a semicircular passage divided it from the mainland, where again a landing was forbidden by a perpendicular precipice. In the unnatural gloom between these formidable ramparts, no break or inlet was to be seen where a boat could have so mysteriously vanished. Yet, when continual grazing of the rocks on either side of the cutter suggested a prudent cessation of oaring, neither sight nor sound was to be seen nor heard to suggest the presence of any living thing. The waters gurgled under the barnacled sea-walls, and as the waves drew back, the tresses of sea-weed dripped and trailed like wet hair.

One of the men uttered an exclamation of superstitious fear. The sense of the ghostly spread, and when the command to back out of the dangerous waterway came it was obeyed with alacrity.

Once outside, the men leaned on their oars, while Lieutenant Larkin stared unbelievingly at the Bull Rock and the cliffs before him.

"It's a trick!" he exclaimed.

The Vanishing Smuggler

What he did not say was that the truth had suddenly dawned upon him. He was at the door of the Heather Bloom mystery, and all that was needed was the magic sesame that would reveal the inside of the whole business.

Of one thing he was certain without knowing why: that Smuggle-erie was in that vanishing boat.

Perhaps it was the reiterations of Horneycraft; perhaps the agitation of Grizel when the possibility was suggested; perhaps his conviction was due to the mere fact that the man left the ship before she dropped anchor; yet, it was more likely that his sense of certainty was the result of the consecutive facts and suggestions. One thing which he did not realize, however, and which was singing confusedly in the subconscious recesses of his mind, was the association of the tune which he had heard Grog-blossom render in the galley and which had thrilled through the dusk as the cutter shot out from the Thistle Down.

He gave the command to row back to the schooner, and his eyes almost involuntarily turned to the bay shore where the road ran through the dark belt of firs. The land at that point was as dark as sepia, but to Larkin's imagination it seemed as if he could discern a shadow, shaped like a man, running.

As the cutter finally shot under the hull of the Thistle Down, he was filled with the notion that he had seen another boat moving from the shore to the starboard of the schooner.

But it was apparently a creation of his eager brain, for when he climbed to the deck and made his way to the cabin, old Jack Cookson arose to meet him with a hearty " What, ho! "

" Come aboard, adm'ral! " said he, waving his hand to an eagle-eyed, sunburned young viking, who stood up with a mischievous devil-take-me grin as Larkin turned to him. " Orders is orders, sir. This is the man, Smuggle-erie."

" Where did you find him? " asked Larkin, meeting the eye of the young sailor with never a tremor of his own.

" On the beach, sir," said the coast-guard, saluting with one finger. " Daffing wi' the lasses, by thunder ! "

Beaten ! The word sparkled, but without malice, in Smuggle-erie's eyes, as clearly as if he had chuckled it. Ben Larkin swallowed his pride with difficulty. Then, acting upon impulse, he held out his hand; for at the first glance, the man in him had recognized the man in Smuggle-erie. And as the two men gripped, it was with an unspoken understanding of mutual appreciation and mutual war.

CHAPTER IV

" GROGBLOSSOM," Smuggle-erie said next morning, " I'm going ashore. How do I look? "

He gave himself a little shake to make his shore togs set straight, and pulled his usually mobile face into the fixed smile of a portrait. Grogblossom came out of the galley, wiped his face, and, as he scanned the young viking before him, drew his mouth corners into the curves of his cheeks in the effort of judgment.

" Ye'll do! Ye'll do! " he finally announced, nodding his head. And at that Smuggle-erie's pose relaxed. " It's a bonny hanky," observed Grogblossom, referring to the spotted kerchief, which Smuggle-erie had spent a good half-hour tying carefully into a careless knot. " Ye'll hae dressed yersel' to visit yer Uncle Giles, I tak' it," added Grogblossom, with a twinkle of his little pig eyes, for Smuggle-erie's attire was in the nature of an event.

" Of course," said Smuggle-erie, grinning. " I'm going to sit on his counter and help him brush the flies off the cheese. Poor man, he's lacking sleep since he forgot to file the edge off a guinea he gave the Laird."

" My respecks to the lass," said Grogblossom, and added thoughtfully, " if ye should happen t'see her."

" I will that," laughed Smuggle-erie, dropping down the rope ladder to the skiff alongside.

" Man," said Grogblossom, lazily leaning over the gunwale, " I weesh ye'd tak' that Red Heid an' have him get his hair cut. It bothers me."

" He has something else on hand," said Smuggle-erie with a wink, " and I'm thinking that with blue-jackets and Horneycrafts and brand-new admirals, Red Mole and the wheen of us'll have our hands full for a while, leastways till this schooner clears. So long, Groggy. Keep sober."

And away shot the skiff over the calm morning waters of Morag Bay, impelled by Smuggle-erie's lusty arms. Grogblossom watched the knifelike split of the water in the skiff's wake.

" That young," he sighed, " and that wickit. Sae fu' o' hope an' strength an' a' life afore 'im. Losh, who's yon in the ither skiff? " he said aloud, as Smuggle-erie's little craft shot across the bows of a similar one, rowed by a young man in gray tweeds. " It looks like yon lufftenant, but he's cast off his brass buttons. Might as weel. Sodgers an' sailor-sodgers is cuddies, chasin' after evildoers wi' brass bands and brass buttons and brass tiliscopes an' blue an' green lichts. Losh! look at that young deevil, wavin' his hand to the lufftenant as if he'd been at dinner wi' him the night before, instead o' runnin' for his very life!"

Grogblossom sighed, and the ever-ready sentimental tear trickled from his left eye.

" That's the way o' him. Pullin' the deevil's tail, as ye might say—puttin' a match to gunpowder t'see if it'll blow up. But it's the way o' youth—the way o' youth! It's a wunner to me how bairns grow up alive, what wi' fallin' doon-stairs, tumblin' in ponds, eatin' sour apples, an' sich-like. But it's the way o' youth—the way o' youth!" And Grogblossom, completely overcome by the appalling optimism of some of God's creatures, waddled into the galley and, having reconnoitered the deck, larboard and starboard, helped himself to a pan of grog and settled down in reverie.

Smuggle-erie, in the meantime, shot past Lieutenant Larkin, whose presence in civilian attire and in Jack Cookson's skiff, was as large print in an open book to him.

" A fine morning, adm'ral!" he hailed.

" Very fine," Larkin replied, feathering his oar calmly as he passed across Smuggle-erie's track.

" There's good flounder spearing in the bay!" shouted Smuggle-erie.

" Thanks; I'm after smugglers ! " was the candid
retort.

Smuggle-erie laughed, wished him luck, and presently his skiff was out of earshot. When the young
sailor beached his boat, he shook the folds out of his
breeches, smoothed his jacket, gave his kerchief a
dainty wiggle, and set off through the one and only
street of Morag, waving his hand to passers-by and
receiving many a cheery salute; for Smuggle-erie was
a favorite.

There was that about the lad which was lovable,
although in the very reckless good-humor for which
he was liked, a shrewd judge would have marked a
character whose ruling principle was the line of least
resistance. He loved that which loved him, and hated
that which caused him discomfort.

In appearance, he was all of a sailor, as he is drawn
by the idealist, and this was due, probably, to the
fact that he was something more than a sailor.
Neither he nor any man aboard the Thistle Down but
carried himself with an air of independence not to be
remarked in your true seaman before the mast. There
was nothing of the hang-dog air which comes from the
haunting fear of the mate's fist. Smuggle-erie's car-
riage was that of a man who loved his employ, and his
quick eye and square brow indicated that his employ
was not all of the hand and back. And aside from
all this, there was a certain air of nobility about the

youth's mannerisms which compelled attention. In
the middle of his irresponsibility, it would flash out in
a glance of the eye, or in a sudden fleeting expression
of his ever-changing face.

His first stop in the village was at Giles Scrymegeour's shop, a half-store, half-office, half-warehouse.
Bales and barrels of flour, fish, hides, liquors, and
what-not, which were being landed from the schooner,
strewed the bit of paving before the place. In the
middle of the confusion Old Scryme danced about,
scolding, directing, nosing, and grumbling. As
Smuggle-erie hove in sight, the old miser tried
to appear as busy as he could, for ever since
a certain night, twelve years before, the situation between guardian and ward had changed, and
Scryme nursed a silent hatred, not unmingled
with fear, of his loud-talking, reckless-tongued
" nephew."

Smuggle-erie, on the other hand, cared no more for
the old scoundrel than for a dead snake. With an
irreverent " Morning, nunky!" he sailed into the
shop and vaulted over the counter. Down on the old
iron box he sat, and taking a gully-knife from his
pocket, began to cut chunks from an adjacent cheese
and cram them into his mouth.

" That's good cheese, nunky," said he.

" Be canny wi't, man!" Old Scryme protested.
" Ye'd think I got it for nothing."

The Vanishing Smuggler

"Next to nothing, nunky. This is what you call Gowdy cheese, is it no?"

"Go away," grumbled Old Scryme. "Can ye no see I'm full of beez'ness?"

"I'm not bothering you," said Smuggle-erie, taking several apples from a barrel, squeezing them into his pockets, and digging his teeth into one.

"Wha gied ye permeession tae eat into ma stock-in-trade like that?" whined Giles Scrymegeour.

Smuggle-erie stared at his "uncle" for a moment, his eyes wide with mock astonishment.

"Permeession? Permeession!" he gasped, then burst out in a roar of rich laughter. "Nunky! Nunky! You'll be the death o' me."

"Aye, will I, some o' the days!" snarled the old man.

"That's strange," said Smuggle-erie, reaching out his hand and taking a fine silk scarf off the counter. "D'ye ken, nunky, I mind when I was a wee bit lad and slept in the garret up-stairs, I used to think how some night I'd crawl down and slit your throat—that's a pretty kerchief, nunky. How'd it suit me? —and after that, force open your old iron box here and take all your guineas and give all the papers and things back to the poor folk you squeezed 'em from."

"Ye—ye—oh, ye rapscallion!" hissed Old Scryme, as his dutiful ward stood up before a cheap looking-

[52]

glass and proceeded to tie the silk scarf in place of
his own more modest kerchief.

" Was it a viper I nursed in ma basom? " cried
Giles Scrymegeour. " Oh, ye—ye—me that tuk ye
oot o' the poorhouse, where ye'd ha' been brought up
on skilly an' water, an'——"

" Say, nunky—honest now! Why did you take me
out of the poorhouse? Wasn't it after ye'd skinned
my old man to the bone that your conscience got the
better o' ye? "

" Skinned yer father to the bone? " shrieked the
miser. " It was beez'ness, I tell ye, pure beez'ness,
and it was nae fault o' mine if yer father was a fool! "

Smuggle-erie's face never changed at the mention
of what would have roused many a man's blood. He
had never known his father, or his mother. Sometimes he wondered idly if it was really a convenience
to have parents; but never having known or dreamed
of any tie that would not have brought hated restraint with it, he had long ceased to trouble himself
as to the ethics of the business.

" It was kind of you to take care of me in my in-
fant years, nunky," said he, standing back to see how
the scarf looked.

" Kindness! " whined Old Scryme. " It was
charity—charity! "

" Aye, aye! " said Smuggle-erie, helping himself to
a pocketful of tobacco plugs; " as Grogblossom would

say, ' Charity suffereth long and is kind.' By-by, nunky! I'm off to see Grizel, and if the breeze is in the right quarter, there's going to be a wedding in Morag, and then nunky is going to do the handsome by his little nephew—eh, nunky?" And the disrespectful young rascal poked Old Scryme in the ribs in a way that nearly made the miser faint.

" Easy, lad! Easy!" he screamed, for if there was one human trait about Giles Scrymegeour it was that he was ticklish. But he turned his hysteria to account, for he suddenly said confidingly to his ward:

" Aye, aye, lad—aye, aye! I have nae word to say agin' the lass. She's a right sens'ble girl—an' thrifty, sir—thrifty! If ye marry her, Dickie, lad, I'd——" He stopped before he committed himself to a promise. " There's nae sayin', lad, but Uncle Giles might come doon handsome. Imphm!" And the old rogue grinned and poked Smuggle-erie in the ribs.

" Nunky's very kind," said Smuggle-erie in his inimitable way. " Very thoughtful, too, is nunky. Once Smuggle-erie was married to Grizel, it would be a family affair, in a manner of speaking—hey?" And with another pass at Old Scryme's ribs he marched out, leaving his " uncle " fuming with sudden rage to think that his little scheme to tighten his grip on Captain John Grant was so patent to the shrewd Smuggle-erie.

That young disrespecter of persons sallied along

the village street, with the looted kerchief fluttering
in the breeze. Everybody had a word for him, especially the lasses, most of whom would have given a lot
for Smuggle-erie's eye. But Smuggle-erie's pole-star
was further out of the village, in a little cottage set
in the middle of a kail-yard. There was a flagstaff a
few yards from the front door, and at the base of it,
on a rude circular bench, sat Grizel.

"What, ho! Sweetheart!" he hailed. "Catch!"
And he tossed an apple over the gate to her. Out
went her hands. The apple slipped through them
and landed in her lap.

"Miss!" he cried. "What ever would a lass do
without skirts?" And he gathered her up in his
arms and gave her the quick peck on the cheek of a
lover who is not very deeply involved.

"Have another apple, lass. Stolen apples always
sweeter, ye ken. Grizel, if you say the word, I'm
ready to marry you."

"Oh, yes?" was all she said.

What could she say? Not that she had any great
objection to marrying Smuggle-erie, but, to a girl,
marrying is one of the great things in life, and any
girl is justified in feeling disappointment that the
matter should be broached and dismissed in the toss of
an apple.

"Don't you want to marry me?" he asked, produc-
ing an apple for himself.

"I'm no in the least particular," said she. "And as long as a girl feels that way, I'm thinkin' there's no great hurry, Smuggle-erie."

There was a little tinge of bitterness in her tone, and her lover was quick to notice it. He turned and looked straight into her face—into her brown eyes. Before his keen, burning gaze, something akin to hero-worship swept through her veins. There was none like Smuggle-erie in Morag. He was the prize. Besides, he was a sailor, and handsome, and strong, and he carried all his matters, even his love-making, with such cool confidence that it was difficult not to go with the rush of him.

"Come, lass, ye love me, don't you?" as if such a doubt were hardly worthy of discussion.

"Oh, yes—of course," was the quiet response.

"Maybe ye like somebody better. Who could it be, now?" he said, addressing an invisible third person. "There isn't a better man for my age in the parish. If you think so, show him to me, Grizel, and him and me will have it out oursel's. Maybe it's the young adm'ral wi' the brass buttons."

"That it is not," said Grizel with a laugh. "Grizel Grant's not for the likes of him." ·

"Oho! That's it, eh? Brass buttons!" Smuggle-erie mocked. "Grizel Grant's not for the likes of him? Then she's not for the likes o' me, for I'm as good a man."

Grant's Confession

There was a little fling of anger in his tone. She put her hand upon his head and crumpled his curling, fair hair.

"Dear old Smuggle-erie! Of course, I'll marry you—when it's time. But you mustn't be jealous like that."

"Me jealous!" he protested.

"Why, you are!" said she. "But I'm not such a fool as some lasses to give my heart to a man because he wears brass buttons and gold lace. But, Smuggle-erie, it's natural, is it no, for a lass to like it?" As she was speaking, Smuggle-erie was quite unconscious of the fine silk kerchief which he had been at such pains to tie around his neck.

"All right, lass!" he cried, tossing his head and dismissing the passing cloud at will. "Give us a kiss."

He flung his arm round her neck in true sailor fashion, and planted a kiss on her cheek with a loud smack.

"Smuggle-erie!" cried a deep voice from the cottage.

"Aye, aye, sir!" replied the lover, jumping to his feet.

Captain John Grant stood in the doorway of the cottage. His eyes were heavy, his face pale, and his brow lowering. It was easy to see that he had passed a sleepless night. He beckoned Smuggle-erie with a toss of his thumb over his shoulder, and said:

" Grizel, haven't you a bit to do this morning? "

The captain led Smuggle-erie into the parlor of the cottage, locked the door, and walked to the window with the remark:

" This is not the time for that sort of fooling, lad."

Smuggle-erie shrugged his shoulders and sat down in a chair by the fireless hearth, for it was still warm weather.

He gave the captain a curious glance as he noticed that Grant was staring through the window with his hands behind his back.

" Aye, aye, sir? " he suggested, after a long silence.

" See here, lad," said Grant, turning around suddenly and beginning to walk up and down the room, " I'm glad you've come up this morning. I was wanting to have a talk with someone—yourself for choice.

" I've known you twenty years, lad. Twelve years ago that mistake o' nature, called Giles Scrymegeour, would ha' drowned you like a blind kitten ower the Bull Rock, if I hadn't had a word to say. Ye needn't thank me for that. It might ha' been as well for you if I'd let him have his way."

The man stopped short in his sea-watch tread and rapped his knuckles on the table in the gesture so characteristic of him when strongly moved.

Grant's Confession

"Smuggle-erie, I'm sick of it! Ashamed of it! I looked through the window a minute ago and saw you and that poor lass on the bench, and I was more ashamed of it than ever. Not that it is my mind, Smuggle-erie, that you should marry my lass, Grizel. I do not say 'aye' or 'no' to that, for there is no time for it now. You're as good a lad as any I know, and a great deal better than most, but——"

He stopped, confused. He had lost the drift of his words in his agitation and eagerness to get them out.

"Smuggle-erie, I'll tell ye something," he began again, his voice deep with the thing that was gripping at his heart. "Ye mind one night last week in the channel, I threw Grogblossom down the companion? (It's all right now. I gave him a pound of tobacco). But no doubt you wondered at it. I am a hard man, but not a violent one. Twelve years ago on that very night I saved your neck, lad, in the lodge by the Laird's gate, and half an hour later, lad, I held my ain lass's hand, my wife, Smuggle-erie —and——

"I can't tell it to ye, lad. I'd make a bairn o' myself. But while I don't say it killed her, it helped, it helped!"

Smuggle-erie shifted uneasily in his seat. Grant walked to the window and looked out. The landscape was bright with the autumn sunshine, yet he saw nothing but a blur. He began to speak without turning his head. His voice was quiet, but there were pauses in his speech.

" After she died, I went bad. Before that I had pursued the business as an honest man, for nothing could teach me—convince me—that a government had a right to tax a people for its food, its drink, its clothing. But after she died, I went at it like a madman. I loved the very worst of it. It helped me forget. Our very name was a terror, for the daring of what we did at times.

" I hadn't meant to tell you this, lad—I mean, all this. But it's too big a thing to let out in driblets. It's like a leak, lad—Tut! What am I saying?

" Three years ago that lass was playing on the doorstep—just playing. I don't know what it was—maybe the way she tossed her hair back, or something —but it's been like a nightmare ever since. I'm not a religious man—Heaven forgive me for even speaking of it—but it's a weight on my soul, black as that soul is, and—I've determined to end it."

" You mean, you'll retire? " suggested Smuggle-erie.

" It's a mild way to put it," sneered Grant. " I mean that the Thistle Down will not leave port again with John Grant as master. The fear of death is on me, man—not the physical fear—but the horror, the shame of my girl's eyes. I saw it last night. Something happened on the schooner. You know what. The strain would have melted iron, and I cried out in my agony. Her hand was on my arm, lad. And when I cried out, she looked at me—and I saw what I swear I will not see in her eyes again for all the world."

Smuggle-erie started up, roused by the man's vehemence. He looked at the white, drawn face of the giant before him and wondered.

"Captain," he said, "you've played the game too long. Take a rest. I'll take the ship out Sunday week if the stuff's ready. You know me."

"I know you, lad," said Captain Grant, a quaver of regret in his voice. "I'd trust you to the last card. But I've spoken the word. The Thistle Down has made her last trip under me and mine. As for you, y'are a free man, but if you engage again in the contraband, independent of me—" he lightly rapped the table with his knuckles—" you are no man for my lass."

Smuggle-erie made no response. It is probable that the whole thing was beyond his complete understanding. He could understand, in a measure, the man's sorrow over the loss of his wife; he could, too, understand his fear of Grizel's scorn; but what he failed to grasp in any degree was why the smuggling exploits *should* have killed his wife; why they *should* arouse Grizel's scorn; why, in short, there was anything to be ashamed of at all in cheating his majesty's revenue. Was not his majesty's revenue an institution which it was every man's duty to cheat?

But one thing Smuggle-erie was shrewd enough to see at once. Grant's nerve had failed. Whether the skipper feared for himself, or for the lass, Smuggle-erie did not trouble to think; he only saw as clearly as daylight that the coming of the naval lieutenant and his men to reënforce Horneycraft and the regular coast-guard, was the finishing touch to the man's remorse.

Grant was distrustful of Scrymegeour, too, and well he might be. They were safe as long as they kept their mouths shut and their nerves taut, but let one of their number show the white feather at the first shot, and the whole gang was in peril.

"It certainly was a tight squeeze," said Smuggle-erie with a shrug. "We could hear their breathing, and they could have heard ours if we hadn't held it. But a miss is as good as a mile."

"But after last night, do you think they will let us rest?" asked Grant sharply. "Not if I know the revenue, or judge a young officer who has a reputation to make. If it was Cookson or any old-timer who is all talk and no active zeal, I would snap my fingers, but unless I'm a fool, that young officer is grubbing around the rock at this minute, and he will keep on grubbing until he finds out what has become of that boat."

" You're a good guesser," said Smuggle-erie, smiling. " He went exploring this morning in old Jack Cookson's skiff."

The announcement had a bad effect upon Grant. He gripped the edge of the table and stared at the young sailor.

" So—already!" he almost groaned. " You saw him?"

" He'll find nothing," said Smuggle-erie assuringly. " It is full tide. Now, if he'd taken a lamp last night—he might have seen wonders."

The captain sighed his relief and went back to the window.

" Come to think of it, though," added Smuggle-erie, " I think I'll go and clear the coast."

" Do, man—do!" Grant pleaded. " There must not be a sign—not a sign."

Smuggle-erie arose and prepared to go. As he passed through the parlor door, he glanced back at Captain John Grant. The big sea-master was again staring out of the window, and the younger man thought he heard him saying, half to himself:

" So! They could hear them breathing—hear them breathing!"

CHAPTER V

WHEN Lieutenant Ben Larkin, rowing across the
bay in Cookson's skiff, passed Smuggle-erie, as the
young sailor was rowing ashore, he felt amused at
their passage of words, but more amused at Smuggle-
erie's gay attire. Whatever position toward each
other fate had decreed for them, the lieutenant would
have been willing to admit that he, at least, bore no
ill-feeling toward his opponent. He wondered what
Smuggle-erie meant by " good flounder-spearing."
It was sarcasm, of course, for Smuggle-erie must
know where the skiff was bound for.

Larkin, on his side, did not need to be told Smuggle-erie's destination. The jaunty angle of the sailor
cap and the gayety of the fluttering kerchief, con-
jured before the lieutenant's mind the face of Grizel,
a young lady in whom Larkin himself felt a growing
interest, not altogether unalloyed with suspicion.

For himself, he adopted no subterfuge, but rowed
toward that point of the Bull Rock where he had last
seen the smugglers' craft. This was on the side of
the rock farthest from Morag village. The height

[64]

of the Bull Rock itself and the landward cliffs obstructed all but a very small view of the passage at either end.

At that time, indeed, Ben Larkin was not sure that the rock was an island. From such inquiries as he had had time to make since his interest was aroused in the matter, he had learned only that no boats ever went there. It was too dangerous at low tide, and at high tide the water barely covered the reefs.

Besides that, it was an uncanny place. There was the legend of the black bull, of course, and not long before a boy had been drowned there and his body had never floated ashore. Between the reefs in the narrow passage, the water sank to a great depth, and if it so happened that a storm rose when the tide was half-full, the people of Morag could hear the water booming as it was forced into these rockpots, and see it spout high in the air as the pressure was relieved.

As Ben Larkin shipped one of his oars and prepared to paddle with the other, the evil name of the place seemed a libel for once. There was an enchantment about the majestic, silent gray walls, with their ancient, gray sheathing of barnacles; the darker islet rock with its smooth, slippery, water-worn sides, draped with slimy tresses of sea-grass; and between them the smooth, dark winding lane of still water.

The lieutenant drew a deep breath of admiration,

and stood up in the boat with his dripping oar-blade raised above the water. For a moment he was part of the picture. It seemed a desecration to b.eak the silence of this sea-temple, or to ruffle its carpet of still waters. He dropped on his knees and rested his chin on the gunwale of the skiff. Only a few inches below the surface, the fangs of the reefs protruded from either side of the passage, like the green teeth of a giant about to close. Between them one could look down through fathoms into the dim sea-light of mystic depths.

It was with a sense of irritation at worldly affairs that he finally recalled the business on hand. He took up his oar and paddled into the inner recesses of the waterway. He passed right through and came out at the northern end, without having seen anything to explain the mystery of the vanishing smugglers. True; it was possible that, even as he had navigated the entire length of the passage, so might the smuggler craft have done. But this was not probable, for the vanished boat, in that case, must have landed between the rock and Morag. This ruse could hardly have escaped the detecting eyes of Horneycraft, even if the score of other onlookers had seen and kept silent.

Larkin was satisfied that the trick—whatever its nature—had been played between the end of the passage at which he had entered and the one at which he now made his exit. He retraced his course through the passage, pausing every few strokes of the paddle to examine thoroughly the rocks on either side, above and below the water.

He reflected that it was now high tide and that some inlet which had escaped observation in the darkness of the previous night might now be submerged. But against this idea was another. If there was aught in the nature of a cave which had swallowed up the smugglers, it seemed certain that it must be flooded. To be sure, the incident of last night had occurred at a lower tide. As he gazed over the side he wondered if, on her previous arrivals, it had been the habit of the Thistle Down to drop anchor at low tide.

Toward the center of the waterway, Larkin noticed that the depth increased and, also, that at this point the tooth-like rows of reef were absent. In fact, the sea here receded under the landward cliff in a manner suggesting that undermining which, among the rugged formations of the west coast of Scotland, has produced so many sea-caves. It was barely possible that at low tide there might be ingress to some hiding-place here. But to make the idea worthy of entertainment, it was necessary also to grant that there was egress from the cave at the other end, unless the smugglers' lair was, like the sea-monsters', in some black grotto containing a vast bubble of air.

The Vanishing Smuggler

The weird thought fascinated Larkin. He shipped his oar and gazed long and keenly into the gray-green depths. There were black shadows there which might be breaks in the rock, or merely the surface of the rock itself, gloomed by the very distance from the surface.

Then Larkin's heart began to beat rapidly. It was not so much on account of what he saw, although the sea-tresses below the surface and the water itself suddenly began to dance under some strange influence! But to his ears, from some vague direction, came a familiar sound—the first bars of that quaint Scotch song which Grogblossom had whistled:

"Pease brose again, mither, pease brose again!"

Then there was a momentary silence. Larkin's hand gripped the edge of the skiff and he glared into the depths of the sea, for, to his puzzled mind, it actually seemed as if the sound was coming up through the water. His heart almost stood still as he waited for the response which he felt ought to come. It came—fainter than the first notes—more distant —more ghostly:

"Ye feed me like a blackbird, and me yer only wean!"

Larkin felt his hair tingle and his spine creep. With the whistling, the agitation of the sea in-

Whirled into the Unknown

creased. The surface began to hiss and twist and foam all around him, and all at once the skiff spun around like a top.

Larkin sprang to the oars with a cry; but oars were useless in that seething caldron of water. Spinning, rocking, and plunging, the skiff shot now a few yards in this direction; then, encountering another current, it was flung back with a crash of water. The lieutenant, while he had little time to think, was yet conscious that he was in some sort of tidal trap.

He could do nothing now but trust to luck and keep his eyes and wits clear. He sat exactly in the middle of his seat, and with his hands gripping either side of the narrow skiff, strove to keep the balance. But it was in vain. The water seemed to sink, but so suddenly that, to the dazzled eye, it was as if the great tooth-like reefs rose out of the water to close upon the little craft.

At the first grinding crunch of the boat's side upon the rocks, Ben Larkin knew that it was no use depending longer upon Jack Cookson's skiff. The turbulent waters, flinging the boat upon a reef and as swiftly drawing away, left her a deadweight, sliding and falling backward into the caldron. The lieutenant, with less of a prayer than a determination to do his best and die hard, flung himself headlong into the windless storm.

Down he went, with the water bubbling white and

[69]

cool around his face. He struck out in the blinding foam, expecting every moment to reach the surface. There presently came a gleam of sunshine, which was eclipsed as soon as he had seen it; then he found himself once more among the snow-like foam, beating thin bubbles with his hands and choking for air.

Once, twice, he saw the light of day. Then again he was below. What did this mean? He was an expert swimmer, yet he could not keep above water. It was as if a giant had reached up from the sea-depths and was beating him about like a ball, flinging him into the sunlight and dragging him headlong to the depths again. Once more the sunlight flashed in his eyes. He opened his mouth to draw breath and next moment, with his lungs bursting with salt, stinging water, he was whirling under the sea, this time in the green bottom-currents.

This was the end! The thought flashed across his mind, as he was relentlessly flung around like a dead weed. He became possessed with a wonderful calm. He was almost glad that death should be by drowning. Presently he would be one with that underworld over which he had but recently dreamed. He felt the soft wrack brush across his face.

Then came a dull shock through his lungs and he opened his eyes, as he firmly believed, for the last time. Away over him was the gay-green light of God's sunny world, and below him was the dim temple of God's great sea, out of which there suddenly shot, *coming up to meet him,* a long, slender body, surmounted by the face of Smuggle-erie!

With a sense of sudden marvel, Ben Larkin drifted into the eternity of nothingness.

CHAPTER VI

A MAN'S A MAN FOR A' THAT

THESE events, mysterious though they appear, are narrated exactly as they happened and in the order of happening, and, like most mysterious things, are susceptible of ready and natural explanation. There was nothing of the supernatural, as the unlucky Larkin supposed, in the ghostly whistle, the sudden convulsion of the waters, and the submarine appearance of Smuggle-erie.

When the latter left Captain John Grant's house, the uneasiness which had determined him to clear the tracks of the smugglers waxed stronger as he walked away toward the Bull Rock, thinking over all that the skipper had to say.

His uneasiness was not wholly due to fear of the revenue-officers. The worm of physical fear had not yet learned to turn in Smuggle-erie's heart, or conscience. But something—he hardly knew what—had stung the lad's vanity. He was vaguely conscious that he had gone to Grant's cottage with a half-serious intention of arranging a wedding. Somehow, his half-serious intention had gone seriously wrong, and his heathen manhood rebelled. His anger rose when the wind, suddenly filliping the silk kerchief in his face, reminded him of the rest of his gala attire, and for what purpose he had worn it.

Without fully realizing it himself, Smuggle-erie was suffering the childish pang of a first disappointment. Grizel, he suddenly felt, was a very different person to what she had been an hour before. She was further removed from him, both in fact and fancy. The sailor's all-embracing love of the petti-coat had become metamorphosed all at once into a strange respect for the mysteries of the business. His mind, so untutored in the delicacy of love, floundered aimlessly around two facts—that Grant had practically negatived his wedding plan, and that Grizel herself had not seemed very enthusiastic about it.

He went back in his mind over every word of their brief conversation under the flagstaff. He wondered where he could have gained the effrontery to talk about marrying her at all. He wondered, indeed, how he had ever had the courage to kiss her as if she was a pet kitten, and love a bobbin on a string. The blood of shame flooded Smuggle-erie's face and neck, which had never before changed color to anything but the sun and the sea.

Whether he realized it or not, there can be no doubt that Smuggle-erie was at last in love, for every time his mind turned upon Lieutenant Ben Larkin, it was suddenly overwhelmed with gloom. Why, he did not know, or try to imagine, but the jealous eye of unconscious instinct had looked out, and knew how the wind blew.

As he neared the abandoned lodge by the gate leading to Morag Castle, Smuggle-erie cast off his heavy thoughts with characteristic alacrity. He had serious business on hand, and, although his mind occasionally reverted to Grizel, it was keenly alert to that immediate business.

He strolled past the lodge, as if taking a morning walk. His eyes took in every detail of the scenery and the road. Then he stopped and looked around. He was a solitary figure on that road, which ran out of Morag and skirted the coast for miles.

At the point where Smuggle-erie paused, the seaward side arose in a steep, ferny bank, ending abruptly at its highest point, where there was a sheer declivity into the waterway behind the Bull Rock. The precipice extended for several hundred yards in either direction, sinking gradually into tumbled rocks and sandy beaches. In heavy weather, the surging waves in the waterway below cast showers of water right over the cliff into the road, which would be flooded at times, for days together.

On the landward side of the road where Smuggle-erie was standing was the old crumbled gate of Laird

A Man's a Man for a' That

Halliday's grounds and, beside it, the ruined lodge. From this, it may be judged that the Laird's estate was not in the best of order. It was, in fact, in a state of disrepair or overgrowth, which the Laird was either too mean to observe, or disregarded for private and personal reasons. The castle itself, strange to say, was a fine old building, and well-ordered, too.

Smuggle-erie, having satisfied himself that both he and the gardener's lodge were unobserved, walked straight toward the door of the deserted building, at the same time whistling, rapidly and softly, the first bars of "Pease Brose Again, Mither," the second line of which came like an echo from somewhere in the vicinity of the ruin.

The young sailor, after another glance around, stepped into the lodge and sat down on a broken chair. Presently a little square patch of the floor was slowly raised and a shock of red hair and a pair of bloodshot, ferret-like eyes appeared.

" Is't yersel'? " whispered a voice, with a quaver of fright in it. " Man, but ye gie'd me a fright that time ! "

" What's frightening *you*, Red Mole? " said Smuggle-erie. " Is it your conscience? "

" Wheesht ! " said the Red Mole, looking strangely like his sobriquet as he peered out of the dark, underground cellar. " Ye're that reckless, man."

"Heave up that hatch, m'lad. There's a king's gentleman spearin' flounder in the waterway."

"What's that ye say?" gasped the Red Mole, flinging up the trap-door and cowering back into the gloom of the hole which was revealed. "A king's man, an' you whistlin' oot there like a mavy. Come awa' doon, man, an' shut the hatch—shut the hatch!"

"Ye old rat!" Smuggle-erie said, with smiling scorn. "Drop a pin an' ye scurry into your hole. But mind the ferret, man, the blue ferret wi' the gold breast. He hunts rats, moles, weasels, and smu——"

The trap-door closed gently over Smuggle-erie's head, and there was silence in the haunted lodge.

Down below, Smuggle-erie squatted on a case of wine and surveyed the Red Mole's quarters, which were filled with miscellaneous merchandise of a contraband nature.

"Making yourself happy, I see," Smuggle-erie said with a nod toward a barrel, upon which rested a bottle and a horn cup beside a lighted tallow-dip.

"Aye, man," whispered the Red Mole, as if an excuse was asked for. "It's the damp, ye ken— drip!—drip!—drip a' the while, an' dribblin' doon the wa's, an' the sea washin'—washin' a' the time. It makes a man feel cauld."

In the old days the place in which Smuggle-erie and the Red Mole sat had played many a part in clan and border warfare. At one time it had been used as a sea-escape from the castle, but time and the undermining of the waters had caused a collapse of the greater part of the passage. The sea-end, however, was still clear and presented a weird aspect at that moment. The tide was full, and the sea, covering the mouth of the cave, flooded to its own level inside. The floor of the rock lair slanted downward into a long black pool, in the bosom of which the waters brightened into the green of daylit water. From the blackness of the inner cave one could sit and watch the fish coming to the mouth, swimming slowly in a short distance, then whisking out again as if in distrust of the candle-eyed monster that dwelt in that underground gloom.

" Ye'll hae a dram yerself? " the Red Mole suggested.

Smuggle-erie looked at the fiery-headed, red-eyed animal before him and refused with a gesture of disgust.

" It's guid whusky! " protested the Red Mole, holding up the bottle with a shaky hand, ready to pour the dram.

" And cheap," said Smuggle-erie. " But a look at you's enough to turn any man from the stuff."

The danger signal of a drunkard's nervous ferocity flashed in the Red Mole's eyes.

" *Let—me—be!* " he suddenly yelled.

" There it is, ye see," observed Smuggle-erie coolly.

" You're about as safe as a loaded gun in a hot oven. Sit down, ye fool, and listen to me. Keep your temper for them that's afraid o' ye! "

The Red Mole glared at him for a moment, his hands twitching and his yellow teeth flashing over his dry lips; then he sat down, pale and trembling, under the force of the superior brain.

" Can ye no mind yer ain beez'ness? " he grumbled.

" Listen to me," said Smuggle-erie. " If the Cot-house stuff is to get through, we—especially you—have to keep a clear head."

The Red Mole flashed the danger signal again, but said nothing. Smuggle-erie continued:

" This stuff has to be cleared out of here as soon's it's dark. There's a pack of hounds smelling around——" Smuggle-erie broke off with a cry—
" What's that? "

He was staring at the long, black pool, where the figure of a man could be seen aimlessly flinging about in the undercurrents at the mouth. The arms and legs of the figure drooped helplessly, and the man's head tumbled limply about as he spun in the water.

" Somebody caught in the ebb! " yelled Smuggle-erie, jumping to his feet.

The Red Mole was also on his feet at the first alarm. His face was stamped with the dread of dis-covery, but as his eyes rested upon the man in the green circle of light in the bosom of the pool, he tuined and laid a restraining hand upon Smuggle-erie, who was wrestling with his jacket-buttons.

"Let 'im drown! Let 'im drown!" the Red Mole whispered tensely. "It's the revenue officer. Let 'im drown!"

He clung to Smuggle-erie as he spoke, with a sort of nervous glee.

The young sailor stopped for a moment as he recognized the figure of Larkin. His brows contracted swiftly and his lip lowered dourly, but only for an instant. Then he struck the Red Mole full in his hairy face and rushed down the incline of the cave with a yell.

"Revenue or no, a man's a man for a' that!" and the last word was drowned in the sullen roar of his body striking the water.

The pool was a tossing, foaming caldron for a moment. Then Smuggle-erie emerged, in a confused heap, with the inanimate Larkin. He struggled wildly toward the shallows.

The Red Mole, forgetting in that moment the pain of his broken lip and his own hatred of revenue spies, sprang forward to help. Such is the instinctive good in the worst of us.

In a few minutes Smuggle-erie was on dry rock, with the lieutenant face downward at his feet. The young sailor was panting madly, but the prostrate figure lay white, still, and dripping.

"Roll him over!" gasped Smuggle-erie. "Roll him over again! Stand him on his head now—there! easy, lad. Fegs! I've spoilt my best togs!" he added, with a short laugh.

"I'm thinkin' he's deid," whispered the Red Mole in a tone of relief.

"Never fear," said Smuggle-erie. "He's too good a man for that. Up wi' that hatch an' get him in the open air."

"Ye're daft!" cried the Red Mole. "D'ye no see?"

"Open that hatch, ye rat!" commanded Smuggle-erie.

"It's no fair!" whined the Red Mole savagely. "It's no fair to me an' the ithers. D'ye no see that ye'll hae t'explain hoo ye got him oot o' the tide race; an' ye canna tell."

"An' if he comes to in here, an' sees that contraband!" roared Smuggle-erie. "Open that hatch, ye black-brained sot, an' get him out—quick!"

"I will not!" said the Red Mole with sudden fire.

Smuggle-erie, who had been bending over Larkin, trying to restore his breathing, sprang to his feet with an oath.

He saw a steel blade glint in the dim candle-light, but flung himself recklessly upon the red-haired man. There followed a crash, and both men rolled on the rocky floor of the cavern. The Red Mole's arm flew in the air, but before the steel descended, Smuggle-erie, who was undermost, gave his antagonist a mighty heave and the next moment it was the would-be murderer who was at the other's mercy. Smuggle-erie's fingers clutched the shock of hair, and the cave echoed the hollow bumping of the Red Mole's head on the rock floor.

"Don't! Don't!" moaned a voice piteously.

"What was the knife for?" Smuggle-erie ground out through his teeth.

"Ye dinna understand!" the Red Mole pleaded. "It was no for ye. It was——"

"Ye mean you would have stabbed a half-drowned man!" Smuggle-erie asserted. "I always thought it was in ye. Get up, ye red-haired Satan. Thankee. I'll tak' the knife. Now, open that hatch."

The Red Mole, cowed to submission, scrambled up the ladder and let the diffused light of the lodge fall upon the candle-lit scene.

Smuggle-erie hoisted the lieutenant up to the Red Mole and then himself climbed up. Once all were in the lodge, the Red Mole let down the trap, and again he faced Smuggle-erie, his lips shaking with fear.

"Smuggle-erie!" he pleaded. "Listen to Baldy Currie." He employed his real name. "If that man leaves this place——"

Smuggle-erie turned on him savagely.

"Another word of that," he said, " and I'll may-

[81]

be bury this knife where you'd be the *least* surprised!"

The Red Mole fell back.

"Here! Bear a hand!" said Smuggle-erie. "Up with him—higher on the shoulder. No, let his head hang. Right! A little more to the front. There! Now, open that door, and you keep your mouth for liquor and leave talk to them that's got sense."

With that parting gift of words, Smuggle-erie staggered out into the sunshine with his rival, Ben Larkin, hanging limp across his shoulders. He gained the road and swung off at a half-stride, half-trot, for Morag.

The first house that he came to—that is, the first where comfort and assistance were available—was the cottage with the flagstaff. As he staggered through the gate into the kail-yard, the front door was quickly opened and Grizel rushed to meet him.

"Oh, what is it? Who is it? What has happened?" she cried.

"A friend of yours," Smuggle-erie managed to gasp, staggering manfully under the dead-weight. "Come to stay f'r a week!"

She glanced at the white face on Smuggle-erie's shoulder and gave a little cry of womanly concern.

"It's the young lieutenant! Oh, the poor man! I must get a bed spread!"

Grizel preceded rescued and rescuer into the cottage. Smuggle-erie reeled into the parlor, where Captain John Grant sat brooding in a chair.

The sea-master sprang to his feet as the young mate dropped his burden on the settle by the empty hearth, and stared like a man suddenly bereft of understanding.

Then his eyes shot from the face of the unconscious man to Smuggle-erie.

" What happened? " asked Grant hoarsely.

" Came into the crow's nest, and the crow was in," said Smuggle-erie shortly. " Send for the dominie."

" You mean—man, you don't mean? " and the big skipper's voice was drowned in a gulp of horror.

" I've cut my knuckles already on the red whelp's teeth," said Smuggle-erie savagely. " Send for the dominie, or this man'll die, if he's no dead already."

A great light leaped into the captain's eyes and he walked to the door.

" Forgive me, lad," he said quietly. " Grizel! " he roared through the door. " Put on your bonnet, lass, and run for the dominie."

" Aye, aye, sir! " said Grizel. " I've sent Daft Tommy as fast as he can go. But we'll have to make a bed in the parlor."

She came into the room on tiptoe and slowly approached the figure on the settle. She gazed at Larkin for a moment, standing a few yards back. Then she whispered fearfully:

" Is he—is he living, Smuggle-erie? "

" Aye, lass, I think so—I hope so," said he, averting his eyes.

Her gaze moved to her reckless lover. His chest was bare, and he was wiping the dyed moisture from his neck. Grizel's eyes faltered and dropped to the carpet, where a pool of sea-water was gathering around Smuggle-erie's feet.

" Was't you—was't you that saved him? " she stammered.

" I hauled him out o' the water, if that's what you mean," said he roughly.

Something rose in her throat and her eyes moved with maternal tenderness to the white face on the settle, and then shyly to Smuggle-erie. She began to cry softly.

At that moment Captain Grant's voice sang out:

" Here comes the dominie, lad, and the coast-guard's with him! "

CHAPTER VII

FOR a week after Smuggle-erie brought Ben Larkin to the cottage behind the flagstaff, Morag nestled at the base of the hills and in the cup of the bay, as innocent a spot as a village in a painted canvas.

But where two or three human beings are gathered together in any cause, there must ever flow the stream of human emotions, fast or slow, but still moving to the climax of the individual and the whole. And in Morag a terrible drama was softly, silently, relentlessly, and unseen, moving to the crucial night of Laird Halliday's harvest gathering—a night that is still remembered in Morag.

It was Saturday morning when Smuggle-erie risked his life and saved his honor for Ben Larkin. It was Sunday morning when the lieutenant came to a full realization of what had happened to him and what had been done for him. The old bell of the parish church was humming in the Sunday stillness, when he awoke, after a long, refreshing sleep, and lay for a while wondering where he was and how he got there.

[85]

The Vanishing Smuggler

The parlor of the skipper's cottage was a bright,
sunny room, and Larkin's eye appreciated in a
moment that he was in the home of a seafaring man.
Besides the ordinary furnishings, there were decora-
tions collected from abroad—sunfish, sharks' teeth,
carved gourds, ray-swords, and other salty suggestions. Over the fireplace, too, was a crude paint-
ing of a schooner, which Ben Larkin at once recognized as the Thistle Down. In the lower part of the
frame were a couple of brass hooks supporting a very
ancient telescope; while underneath was a master's
certificate framed in plain oak.

When Grizel Grant stole into the room for a peep
at the patient, Ben was delighted, but not surprised.
He had already made up his mind that he was in
Captain John Grant's house. It occurred to him
that the situation was a bit anomalous. If his suspicions of Smuggle-erie proved correct, they must
naturally extend to the master of the Thistle Down.

Grizel stood looking down into his open eyes for
a moment before she realized that he was awake.
Then she stammered something about being very glad,
and went away to call the skipper, who presently returned alone and asked Larkin how he felt.

"Astonished, that's all," was the reply. It was
given in a voice the weakness of which was a further
astonishment to the patient.

"Good!" said the big sea-master. "That's the

way with drowning. It either kills or does little harm."

" So I was drowned? " said Larkin. " Yes, I remember——"

He paused and looked inquiringly at the captain, whose face took on its steel-trap expression.

" I remember seeing Smuggle-erie coming up through the water to meet me." He stopped and turned an appealing eye on the skipper. " I'm afraid I'm still a little light-headed, but I distinctly remember—— It was very odd. . . . Oh, rubbish!" he added wearily.

" I wouldn't bother my head about what you— about how you felt when you were in the water," said the captain. " You had better go to sleep again."

He moved as if to leave.

" No, I'm all right," said Larkin. " Who was it saved me? "

" Dick Scrymegeour," the captain replied, turning in the middle of the floor.

" Who's he? "

" He's best known as Smuggle-erie," was the reply.

" Oh!" After a pause, Ben Larkin added: " So it *was* Smuggle-erie? . . . I would like to see him."

" As soon as you are fit," said the captain. " Better sleep, my friend. It's the best cure." This time, with a smile, he turned and went out of the room.

The Vanishing Smuggler

Larkin did not sleep at once. So it *was* Smuggle-erie! It was, then, not a dream—not the hallucination of a drowning man. Smuggle-erie *had* come up through the water to rescue him.

The matter lingered in his mind, though he attempted to banish it as being a poor show of gratitude to the man who had saved his life. Yet it was his duty. His duty? To turn a man's brave act into evidence that would put him in jail?

Dick Scrymegeour—Smuggle-erie? Probably he was related to Giles Scrymegeour, the trader to whom the Thistle Down was consigned. Ah! Possibly——

"This won't do," thought Ben Larkin. "I'll drive myself to a fever."

He turned over in bed and looked at the wall, and saw the face of Smuggle-erie coming up to meet him through the green water. Why, then, did the man save him? If, indeed, he was a smuggler; if, indeed, he was—as Larkin suspected—Heather Bloom, why did he not let him drown?

Then he idly wondered whether smugglers were as black as they were painted. Was smuggling such a bad business after all? One thing was certain. They had crossed swords a second time, and again Smuggle-erie had come out victor—distinctly so! And, having settled that, he fell asleep, and dreamed of a nut-brown lass who stood over his bed and looked down into his eyes.

Still Waters Run Deep

Ben Larkin was not more than twenty-six years old. His uniform, of which he was so proud, made him look older. Without it, he looked what he really was—an overgrown lad, with a great deal of sincerity in him. Ever since he had taken up his command in the Coast-Guard Service at Morag, he had been conscious of his extreme youth and inexperience, but never so painfully as now. The knowledge, however, while it was ever with him, whetted his ambition to prove that he could be a man when occasion required.

After church was out, old Jack Cookson put in an appearance and insisted upon seeing " the adm'ral." Here was one, indeed, who unconsciously gave comfort to the young lieutenant, in that the old sea-dog, as Pitt said to Walpole, continued ignorant in spite of age and experience. To the coast-guard, Ben Larkin had communicated none of his suspicions. Horneycraft had communicated all of his, naturally, and to the sum-total of them old Jack Cookson had replied:

" Smugglers aboard the Thistle Down, sir? You are wrong, sir! If there was a smuggler aboard that craft, he wouldn't *dare look me in the face,* confound 'im ! "

Cookson was a sailor, accustomed to swing a cutlass when the enemy was shown him, and none doubted the old fellow's valor ; but it was this very valor that

[89]

blinded him to the possibility of a man not fighting in the open, " like an Englishman, sir ! "

As he stood in Captain Grant's parlor, he was the very picture of what he was—an obsolete but picturesque old hulk, whose principal duty as coast-guard was to strut round like an old turkey-cock with his telescope, white trousers, and blue coat, and with tales of how he lost his left arm at the battle of Trafalgar, to keep alive the naval spirit and general patriotism of the rising generation.

" Aha, m'lad ! " said he, when he had offered the usual solicitous inquiries after health and sleep, " this reminds me of a certain adm'ral of great and glorious mem'ry—God rest his soul and confound the French ! As he lay in the old Victory, sir, a-dyin' of his wounds, he——"

" You mean Horatio Nelson ? " said Larkin gravely.

" Who else, sir ? " snorted Jack Cookson. " Lord Nelson, sir—my old adm'ral. Son of a clergyman he was—a sky-pilot !—what d'ye think o' that? Piloted more Frenchmen to glory in one hour than his father did in a lifetime, by thunder !

" That was at Trafalgar, sir, same engagemint I lost m' left arm—in the sarvice of my country and king, God bless 'im ! I remember it like it was yes-terday, sir. Only a few minutes before he fell, witally wounded, sir, a shot tore off my left arm. I lay on that deck, sir, wishing another shot would take off my head and be done with it. Next thing I sees is my old adm'ral a-bein' carried to the cockpit, sir. You're young, sir—beggin' your pardon, and you won't believe it; but when 'e waved 'is hand to us lads —witally wounded, sir—I forgot I 'ad ever 'ad a left arm, and I sat up, sir, and cheered, by thunder!— *cheered!*

"After that it didn't matter to me, nor to none of us. If we was wounded, so was 'e! Shot and shell? Minded 'em no more'n peas and parsley, sir—*peas and parsley!* Over'ead was the glorious string of signals: 'Hengland expecks this day that every man will do his dooty.' And—we—done it, by thunder! —to a man, sir! I was disabled—lost m' left arm, sir—but I lay on that deck and shouted with might and main: 'God bless King George and *damn* the French!'"

And old Jack Cookson finished his favorite yarn with a battle-roar that brought in Mrs. Martin (the skipper's housekeeper since Mrs. Grant died), who said, with much acidity:

"Wad ye hae the guidness to bear in mind, Adm'ral Cookson, that this is the Sawbath day?"

"What's that?" snorted old Cookson. "What did I do? What did I say?"

"Ye said 'damn the French,'" asserted Mrs. Martin, adding as an afterthought: " Heaven forgie me for repeatin' the vile word."

" Madam," said the coast-guard, rising in all his naval dignity, telescope and all, " far be it from an Englishman to contradict a lady, but I distinctly said ' *confound* the French!' "

" Pardon me, Adm'ral Cookson," retorted Mrs. Martin stiffly, " I am no' dull o' hearin'."

" I appeal to the adm'ral in the cockpit here!" cried Cookson. " Did I say ' damn,' sir? "

" I didn't catch the precise word," said Ben Larkin, highly amused, " but if it wasn't ' confound,' it was a word to that effect."

" There! " snorted the coast-guard, and Mrs. Martin retreated under all sail.

" That silenced her guns, sir," said Jack Cookson victoriously.

Just as the patient began to grow drowsy over the coast-guard's yarns, the dominie put in an appearance.

The two men were as opposite in character, tastes, and learning as a high priest and a cabin-boy. Yet, over a friendly grog and each with a churchwarden clay pipe, they got along together like a pair of ducks. But, when one comes to think of it, they could hardly disagree, seeing that the one never listened to a word the other was saying, only waiting a chance to wedge in a story of his own.

Still Waters Run Deep

"And how does the patient progress to-day?" asked the kind old dominie, after the usual greetings. "Let us hope, well. There have been no symptoms of suffusion of blood in the lungs, I trust, nor have you experienced any great pains in the head? Ah! That is gratifying. You will be well in a few days. Rest is all you need. In extreme cases, where there might have been breaking of the lung cells from strangulation, I might have administered a drug; but nature, my friends, is the sovereign remedy for all ills. We, despite our ever-increasing knowledge, are but servants of the great medico, the master-surgeon, Nature. In the olden times, leeches were applied for reducing the pressure of blood, but modern science has established that blood being a necessary concomitant of physical strength, it was highly desirable that it should be left to thrive the patient. Nature, sir! Nature is the sovereign alchemist."

"That's book-larnin'—book-larnin'!" said the coast-guard. "An' I know it to be facts, sir. Why, at sea there war'n't no folderols about the sick-bay arter an engagement. Nature, by thunder! *Nature done it!* I've seen a doctor sail in an' ampytate a man's leg with a *cutlass*, sir, and that man has the finest wooden leg you ever seen! And main proud o' that leg, too—made out of a mizzen-stump as was shot away in the engagement with Du Grasse. Ship's carpenter turned it out while Rodney was towin' the whole French fleet into Jamaica!—place they make rum, sir."

Then the dominie discoursed on Jamaica and remarkable instances of amputation, and the two old fogies ended by going off arm-in-arm to the coast-guard house, Cookson with his telescope and the dominie with his staff, and the bit of lace falling in old-fashioned grace over the handle. Ben Larkin lay in bed, smiling at the queer pair they made.

When he awoke again, dusk had set in. He felt refreshed, contented, and stronger. Nevertheless, he was comfortable with the comfort that will not be disturbed. It was pleasant to lie there in the soft light of the lamp that had just been set on the table, and watch the glow of it on the hair of the nut-brown lass. She was sitting by the hearth in which the first fire of the season had just been built. It was beginning to sputter with the melodious suggestion of coziness.

"Miss Grizel," he said.

She came to the bedside, and, seeing that he was awake, would have run off, as before, to bring her father or Mrs. Martin. But he detained her.

"You have been very kind," he said.

"I'm sure," she returned, a bit confused, "that we're quite paid for it if your life has been saved. It—it isn't everyone, captain—I mean, lieutenant—who ever gets a chance to—to save somebody's life."

" That's a very deep remark," he said, smiling.

" For a man, maybe," she flashed mischievously.
" A woman, ye ken, must spend a' her life saving."

" Saving men, you mean? "

" In a way. Saving his money for him, if nothing else."

" Miss Grizel," said he curiously, " do you always talk like that? "

" W-why? " she stammered.

" Because I like listening to you."

" I must call my father," she interrupted. " He said I must light the fire, so we could sit by and cheer you up."

" Did you light the fire? "

" Yes."

" And the lamp? "

" Of course."

" A sort of little mother in the house," he suggested.

She turned very red in the face, but it was plain she was not displeased.

" Mother died, why, when I was only five years old," she explained; " and Mrs. Martin reads her Bible on Sundays."

The shadow of the big sea-master fell across the room, and Grizel pulled his armchair into position by the fire. After a few words with Larkin, he sat down; and there followed an awkward pause.

Plainly, the man was ill at ease. And well he might have been. The presence of the revenue officer —indeed, the whole circumstances of the business— seemed like the finger of Providence or a judgment. After a few minutes, Grant looked at Grizel and said:

" It's Sunday, lass. Will ye no play on the harmonium? "

The little organ stood near the improvised extra bed on which Larkin lay, and was so situated that when Grizel sat down at it he could see her profile silhouetted against the firelight, and now and then a glint of pink on her cheek. She silently turned over the pages of the old hymnbook until she came to a favorite piece. Then, with her head quaintly poised and the tip of a little pink tongue peeping nervously from the corner of a pretty mouth, she played for the two men.

For a moment Ben Larkin was happy. The tenderness of sound and scene swept through him. Then he came up short, with a jarring pang, for his eyes suddenly fell upon the drooping, despondent figure of John Grant. The captain was leaning forward, elbow on knee and cheek in hand, staring moodily into the fire. Ben Larkin thought he understood, but he was as sorry for himself as for the big sea-master.

In the middle of Grizel's playing, Smuggle-erie put in an appearance. He was at once overcome with embarrassment. He was not used to quiet socials of any kind, and there was something especially dispiriting about this one. When Grizel's playing ceased, hat in hand, he passed from father to daughter, shook hands in some sort of fashion, and seemed relieved when he found himself talking to Larkin.

" How is it, lad? " he said, with kindly familiarity.

" All well, thanks to you," Larkin replied, shaking hands with him. " You are a man, Smuggle-erie."

" I hope so. If not, there's still time," was the odd evasion of the compliment. " You wanted to see me? "

" Naturally. How did you get me out of that terrible passage? "

" I *didn't* find you in the passage," was the cool response. " The tide drew you out of it and I picked you up elsewhere. Come, don't let's talk about it."

Larkin suddenly felt ashamed.

" I—I didn't mean to—I shouldn't have spoken about it," he stammered. " But I'm grateful. You know that, don't you? I'm grateful."

Smuggle-erie's eyes, twinkling with amusement, looked down into his.

" That's all right, lad. I did my duty, as I expect you to do yours."

Despite the good humor of his eyes, there was a shade of subtler meaning in his expression.

The Vanishing Smuggler

Smuggle-erie sat down and Grizel began another hymn.

The man on the bed heard in a dim way, but his eyes moved from one face to another. Ben Larkin respected Grant, despite his suspicions; he admired Smuggle-erie, despite his convictions; and he was beginning to love Grizel, in spite of himself and the gulf between them.

All four must have blessed the little harmonium, which precluded talk and drowned the silence. All except the innocent Grizel seemed to *hear* the thoughts of the others through the soft music, as the firelight danced mockingly on the faces of the three men. Smuggle-erie fidgeted uneasily in his chair, and his cap seemed an incubus on his knees. His eyes lingered with a puzzled look on Grizel's hair, shifted unhappily to the silent giant by the hearth, and finally fixed on Ben Larkin's face. The young officer was half sitting, half reclining, with his elbow on the pillow, and, for a moment, his gaze was upon Grizel's face. Smuggle-erie saw it, and the next moment his eyes met the lieutenant's—and the hymn ended with a decisive " A-amen."

Smuggle-erie rose, bade them a short good-night, and left the house. Under the flagstaff he stopped. With his thumbs stuck in his belt, he looked back at the lighted parlor window.

The sweet, quiet strains of the harmonium swelled

like some tender passion, and all at once an uncontrollable wave of pagan rage and jealousy burned in Smuggle-erie's heart. With an oath, he swung away toward Morag, and as he walked, he ripped out in savage tone:

" I wish I'd let him drown ! "

CHAPTER VIII

THE NIGHT OF THE HARVEST-HOME

Smuggle-erie's jealousy was not without reason, and he was quick to realize it. Larkin's growing interest, too, could not hide itself much longer from Grizel's eyes, nor from the shrewd perception of the dismayed Captain Grant. But the lieutenant, with creditable delicacy and good sense, returned to the coast-guard station as soon as he was fit to walk, which was on Monday.

For the rest of the week, however, try as he might to avoid it, Larkin found himself, in some way or other, walking with Grizel or meeting with her and passing part of the day in passing the time o' day.

Miss Grizel, daughter of Eve, may have had a hand in this seeming moving of the fates. Indeed, she was displeased with Smuggle-erie. Her old lover had suddenly grown sullen, and when he was with her for more than five minutes, they invariably quarreled. The sense of disappointment which she felt when he tossed her an apple under the flagstaff, presently resolved itself into a kind of resentment at his churlish love-making. Thus the lieutenant held the field almost undisputed.

Like a bull that has charged a shadow and stunned itself on a tree, Smuggle-erie battled with the vague jealousy which had newly come into his experience. Until Grizel entered the game, if his interests had been opposed to those of Ben Larkin, it had never occurred to the young viking that he need fight very hard, such was his confidence in his prowess. But this was a game of which he was no master, and his repeated attempts to score a point failed, or only succeeded in scoring for Larkin. He had one consolation, however, and that was his ability to beat the lieutenant at the game of " smuggle-erie." And beat him at every turn he vowed to himself he would.

It is doubtful, indeed, whether Smuggle-erie was capable of truly loving Grizel, or any other woman. There was much in him that was lovable, or admirable, but the circumstances of his childhood and the nature of his profession all tended to an inoffensive egotism—the self-protective instinct of the fine animal. His jealousy of Grizel's love was—as, indeed, all jealousy is, more or less—merely the sense of being robbed. The difference between Smuggle-erie's jealousy and that of a less self-loving man was the difference between the dog in the manger and the fox that really wanted the grapes.

By the end of the week, when the annual harvest-

home was to take place in the big hall of Laird Halliday's castle, matters had reached a point where something definite was bound to happen. Something *did*
happen that night—many things happened which involved other persons besides Smuggle-erie, Grizel, and
Ben Larkin.

The harvest-home was, next to the New Year's Eve
jollification, the biggest social event in Morag.
From all the countryside came the laird's tenants and
the neighboring farmers to celebrate the homing of
the harvest, was it good or bad. The laird himself
was not a sociable man, although this was ever a matter for surprise to those who saw his jolly, fat face
at his sole annual appearance. He headed the table,
which groaned with hams, haggis, poultry, and other
eatables; danced with Mary, Maggie, and Molly;
drank with Tom, Dick, and Harry, and paid the
piper, both figuratively and literally. Then for
three hundred and sixty-four days he was again a
recluse.

It was a grand night for love-making, eating, and
drinking in the old castle, and Morag was a deserted
village while it lasted. Smugglers were given a holi-
day, for the Coast-Guard Service attended to a man,
led by "Adm'ral" Jack Cookson with his shining
telescope and best uniform. The king's gentlemen
rubbed shoulders and clinked glasses with Heather
Bloom and his daring lads, without knowing or caring

who they might be. The dominie lent an air of venerable distinction to the proceedings, and even Giles
Scrymegeour and Horneycraft had been known to
have a civil word for each other at the harvest-
home.

But this year both Giles and Horneycraft had
other business to attend to. What Horneycraft's
doings were, none ever knew until they were done, and
what Old Scryme's might be, only the Evil Eye could
tell. As a matter of fact, Giles Scrymegeour had
chosen the night of the harvest-home as being highly
suitable for the transaction of a little piece of business which it would have been inadvisable to perform
in public and in daylight.

The harvest-home feast began about five o'clock in
the evening. As soon as it was dark, Old Scryme,
gazing with satisfaction along the deserted street,
closed up his house and shop, and putting the key in
his breast-pocket, mounted the shaggy pony which it
was his custom to ride when business took him to the
hills.

He carefully avoided the vicinity of Morag Castle
or the road leading to it, making a détour in order to
avoid meeting anybody. When he finally emerged
upon the main highway winding up into the hills, it
was pitch-dark, and Giles, leaning nervously over the
pony's neck, whipped up greater speed.

Giles Scrymegeour, it is hardly worth mentioning,

was a poltroon of the veriest depths. His conscience
was bad, and a bad conscience is like having a Jere-
miah for a bedfellow—a constant reminder of evil
things. As Old Scryme rode through the darkness
he was filled with the dread that something—not a
ghost, but something material—was following him.
Of ghosts there were plenty, too. They sat behind
him on the pony, trotted alongside, rose up before the
pony's head, and leaned over Giles's shoulder with
little reminding whispers of things Old Scryme had
done in the past.

To enumerate Giles's virtues, it would be necessary
to employ a process of elimination and then hold a
court of inquiry upon what was left. When he first
came to Morag, the village was Eden before the arrival of the serpent. He loaned money at the beginning, and generously refrained from foreclosing his
mortgages. In this way he swung the sword of
Damocles over the heads of his victims. In time he
opened a licensed tavern. By degrees he tightened
the rack upon Morag, until at the time of this story
he was, in one way or another, master of the village
and keeper of Morag's honor, most of which, neatly
tied with white tape, reposed in the old iron box in
his office. He lived in nightly dread of being murdered, and he never went out after dark unless the
matter on hand were well worth it. The agonies he
endured from his tortured conscience and an in-

stinctive fear of the dark, were often a dear price for what he gained.

He was vastly relieved, therefore, when a light on the hillside about two miles behind Morag told him that his destination was near. He whipped up the pony and pressed on—

> Like one that on a lonesome road
> Doth walk in fear and dread,
> Because he knows a frightful fiend
> Doth close behind him tread.

It was with a sigh of relief that he drew up before the Cothouse Inn and tied his pony to the hitching-post.

The Cothouse was a mountain roadhouse of particularly sinister repute. Parents discouraged their children from walking on the Cothouse road on Sunday afternoon, for it was whispered with horror among the rigid Presbyterians that the inn was the Sunday resort of drunkards and gamblers from the surrounding hills. The nominal proprietor of the place was Baldy Currie, better known as the Red Mole; but rumor had it that Giles Scrymegeour was controller of the till.

The Red Mole spent most of his days upon the sea, and for the most part the public-house bar was managed by Mrs. Baldy Currie, an enormously fat woman, whose favorite tipple was vinegar, and whose tongue was as sour. That vinegar, which she drank in efforts to regain her lost barmaid beauty, was the only womanly trait left in her character. Her son, a tall, muscular, surly youth, was the only law and order in that lawless, disorderly plague-spot. He ruled by terror.

On this the night of the harvest-home the inn was deserted except for the Curries. Mrs. Currie could be heard snoring stertorously upstairs. The air was faintly impregnated with strong vinegar.

The Red Mole greeted Old Scryme with the obsequiousness of hatred and led the way into a back room. Here there was a young man lying asleep on a table. It seemed as if he would never uncurl himself to his full length, when his father roughly awoke him. Then he stood up in his long leather boots and guernsey, and waited for someone else to speak.

" Weel," said Old Scryme, " is't a' ready? "

" Aye! "

" Had we no better see it? "

The tall youth took a key from a nail, while his father, the Red Mole, fetched a lamp.

Archibald, as the son was called, then lifted the shop shutters from their accustomed place on the wall. Behind them was a door into which he slipped the key.

" There ye are," said the Red Mole. " None o' yer public property f'r me. When it's day, there's the shutters, and wha'd think there was a door ahint?

An' then when it's night, an' the shutters are up, there's none to see but me an' mine."

" Aye, aye! " said Giles with a grin.

The son silently waved them into the open doorway and stood on guard as they went below. In the cellar the light of the Red Mole's lamp revealed about half a hundred kegs stacked neatly at the farther end.

" Ye canna wait a wee an' make it mair worth while? " whined the miser.

" Not another day," said the Red Mole decisively, as he set down the lamp. " It's no safe a minnit longer. What wi' that young fool Smuggle-erie turnin' the castle hole into a hospital, an' a long-nosed, whey-faced collector prowlin' ahint hedges——"

" Ahint hedges! " Old Scryme echoed, looking hastily around the cellar. " What d'ye mean? "

" Yon Hoarneycraft man's been pokin' aroon' this place for twa days."

" Horneycraft! "

" Aye, but I'll no hae seen him the day. He'll hae gi'en it up in disgust, like."

" Aye, aye. I'm glad to hear't. Noo, is the cart an' the lads ready for the morrin's night? "

" Aye, aye," the Red Mole replied. " They'll leave on the stroke o' twelve. But what's this I'm hearin' o' Heather Bloom? The lads'll want an answer on that afore they'll risk it."

" Leave that to me," whispered Giles with a grin.

" I hae a wee word that'll send him to sea as quick's Jack Robinson. He's been like that afore, but— wheesht! What's that?"

Giles stopped and stood listening with his fingers raised to the roof. Light footsteps could be heard passing through the public bar.

" It's Archibald, man—just Archibald," said the Red Mole.

" Na, na," whispered Giles, turning very pale. " It's no Archibald. What for wad he tiptoe like that? "

At that Baldy Currie, who knew that his son was a lumbering animal, suddenly made a grab for the lamp. He paused.

The two culprits stood for a moment in breathless suspense. Then came a sudden rush of feet and a fierce oath in Archibald's voice.

" Guid forgie me! I'm trapped!" cried Old Scryme.

" Shut up, ye auld idiot!" the Red Mole snarled, his eyes lurid with the danger-signal. " Another word an' I'll thraw yer neck. Get ahint the barrels— quick!"

Giles Scrymegeour flung his riding-cloak over his face and sprung toward the hiding-place, but before he could conceal himself there came a rumbling and tumbling, and down the flight of stairs rolled Archibald interlocked with the revenue collector, Mr. Horneycraft.

The Night of the Harvest-Home

The moment they reached the bottom of the stairs, Archibald knew that he had his man safe.

He disentangled himself and took up a stand on the stairway where he could bar the enemy's exit.

Mr. Horneycraft, however, had no intention of leaving. He stood up before the Red Mole and bowed in sardonic triumph.

"Ah, Mr. Currie," he sneered. "An unexpected visit, eh? Mr. Scrymegeour, I observed as I came in, was suddenly overcome with commendable modesty. Come out, Mr. Giles Scrymegeour—come out!"

There was a gravelike stillness in the cellar for a few seconds. The lamp in Red Mole's hand shook like a light reflected in moving waters, but the tall youth on the staircase stood there as stiff and expressionless as a Roman soldier.

Then Giles Scrymegeour came from behind the barrels. His face was livid, but if there was any fear in it, it was the fear of desperation.

"Is't yersel', Maister Horneycraft?" he snarled. "It's a braw night—for you!"

"It is, indeed," said Mr. Horneycraft coolly. "I think I will set my official seal upon this cellar and escort you before the nearest justice of the peace."

It must be said for Horneycraft that he showed not a trace of fear. Yet his bravery was not of the kind that is truly admirable. Rather, he was so steeped in his business and so hardened to the desperation of those whom he found guilty of evading the revenue, that it is probable the peril of his situation never dawned upon him.

" An' so ye'll set yer official seal on the place, will ye? " said Scrymegeour. " Mebbe we might set an official seal on yer mouth! "

" Spare your threats, Mr. Scrymegeour," said Mr. Horneycraft loftily. " I've heard threats before."

" Mebbe ye'll no hear them agin," said Giles uneasily, as if he hesitated to utter the words that, once out, could not be recalled.

The figure in the stairway took a step nearer. The Red Mole put down the lamp. Giles gathered courage and support from these movements.

" Ye'll escort us to the nearest justice of the peace, will ye? " Old Scryme rasped out. " Are ye sure that y'are goin' yersel'? "

He, too, crept a step nearer Mr. Horneycraft. All at once he said in an evil, quick whisper:

" An ill day for you, Mr. Horneycraft, that ye recognized Giles Scrymegeour. If there's to be bloodshed in this place the night, be it yer ain an' upon yer ain heid! "

" Na, na! " cried the Red Mole, his terror of discovery getting the better of his animal ferocity. " There'll be none o' that in my hoose. They'd search for him."

Scrymegeour turned upon him like an animal at

bay. He saw with his cunning, ratlike shrewdness that it was the life of the hunted or the hunter. Above all things, he saw that it was chiefly necessary for the safety of Giles Scrymegeour that someone else be a party to the murder.

" Ye're mighty canny, Baldy," he jeered. " Was't no' you that wad hae cut the weazand o' the lufftenant in the cave? "

Mr. Horneycraft pricked up his ears. The Red Mole subsided.

Old Scryme went forward and whispered rapidly in his ear. The hairy monster shook like a leaf in the breeze, and his lips made inarticulate sounds of protest and assent.

Then Giles turned upon Mr. Horneycraft and bade him good-night.

" You cannot leave this place! " cried Horneycraft. " I arrest you in the king's name! The place is surrounded! "

" It's a lie! " the tall youth on the staircase said stolidly.

Horneycraft, who had almost forgotten his late antagonist's existence, turned around with a start.

In that moment Giles Scrymegeour slipped past him. Horneycraft sprang to stop his passage, but Archibald hurled the collector back.

In another moment Giles Scrymegeour had reached the public-house upstairs. As he stood for a moment, dazed with nervous reaction, he heard the stertorous breathing of Mrs. Currie and smelt the taint of vinegar. Stricken with sudden horror, he rushed from the place. He unhitched the shaggy pony and scrambled into the saddle. From within he heard an inner door close with a heavy slam and a rusty key turn in the lock.

The miser lashed the pony into a gallop. About a quarter of a mile down the hill he suddenly remembered that if the crime was to be hidden, his appearance must not be the first thing to arouse suspicion. He drew the pony to a standstill and allowed the half-winded animal to blow. Suddenly conscious of the mountain silence around him Giles turned in the saddle and looked at the dim light of Cothouse Inn.

He wondered what was going on in the cellar under that house. Were they killing him now? How would Baldy do it? Smother him? Stab him?

As his mind danced from one alternative to another, among the still mountains, echoing like the shrieking of a million devils, went the long, wailing cry of a human being in distress.

Giles Scrymegeour, with a gurgling noise in his throat, brought down the lash upon the pony's head. The animal lunged violently, then horse and rider rushed down the hill road in mad flight.

CHAPTER IX

GILES never slowed up until he was on the outskirts of the town. Even then he urged the pony over the same détour at a speed to arouse suspicion. Fortunately for him he met no one, the harvest-home having assimilated most of the population.

It had been Old Scryme's plan, once he had stabled the pony, to go to bed. Suddenly it occurred to him that an alibi was a poor thing if there was nobody to witness it. There was only one move for him to make, and his cowardly soul shrank from it. He must appear at the harvest-home, and that as if he had been there all the time.

Behold, then, the old scoundrel struggling with a white linen shirt, which presently covered as black a heart as beat that night in Morag. When fully dressed he went away swiftly toward the laird's castle, where he presently appeared in conversation with this man and that, seeming at each encounter with his acquaintances to have chanced upon them for the first time, and expressing surprise thereat.

It was a very different scene from the cellar of the

[113]

Cothouse Inn, this big hall of Morag Castle. The fun was in full swing when the miser put in an appearance. The eating-tables had been thrust to the walls or cleared away altogether. On one of them sat Blind Johnny and his blind son, both with their fiddles tucked under chin and dirling away at Scotch dance music. The castle fairly shook with the simultaneous tap of hundreds of feet in the boisterous Highland dances, while the air was split with the exuberant " *Hooch! Hooch!* "

In the middle of the swirl was Smuggle-erie, as master of the floor. His eyes were bright and his face animated with the fire of excitement and pleasure. Not far from him was Ben Larkin, with Grizel on his arm. For once, Smuggle-erie seemed to have forgotten his jealousy, and the way he swung an isolated maid around, when his duties gave him a chance, suggested that one lass was as good as another when it came to a reel.

Around the walls, on the tables and chairs, were the old folk of Morag, all looking on with reminiscent smiles and fondness for their sons and daughters. To see a mother's eyes follow a lass on the floor was to imagine a picture of the dressing before the ball— the old mother's touch on the ribbons and curls and the final approval; while the winking—nudging— chuckling of the old men as the youngsters twirled their partners about was a story in itself.

Love or Duty?

The dominie was there, of course, with his chin well-nigh settled on the handle of his staff, and at his side was the voluble coast-guard. Near him was Captain John Grant.

"And they dare to tell me in the face of this," cried old Cookson, "that there are smugglers in Morag? Why, sir, even if there were—even if there were, I say!—what's the odds, by thunder? All's fair in love and war. This is love, and strike me to'gallants, that lass of your'n, cap'n, is the slipperiest craft in the whole fleet." This, as Grizel swung gracefully past with Larkin. "A trim craft, sir, with a clean pair o' heels, and a noble consort, by thunder! A gentleman and an officer of the king—God bless 'im!'"

"The way o' youth—the way o' youth!" mournfully murmured Grogblossom, who looked more like a pig than ever in his best clothes. "It's a' very fine, but change and decay'll bring wrinkles to them a' and——"

"Tut, tut!" protested the dominie, turning upon Grogblossom. "You speak, as the poet did, my friend, of the roses that to-morrow will be dying, but change and decay do not destroy the sense of the poet's first thought, 'Gather ye rosebuds while ye may.' Life, my friend," he added with a paternal smile upon Grogblossom, "is an experience. We live it but once, so that each of its seven ages comes to us

[115]

as a novelty. Even the grave, from which none has returned to speak, may be, for all we can tell, another novelty."

" That's book-larnin', by thunder—book-larnin'! " cried Cookson, while Grogblossom drifted away, shaking his head. " Talkin' o' experiences an' novelties, sir, what you say is proved by facts. I knew a man —bo'sun o' the old Urgent—as was a-haulin' at the gaskets when a rope gave way an' he fell from the mizzen-tree straight to the deck. Was 'e killed? No, sir! The old Urgent rolled on a sea and the man fell into the ocean. Was 'e drowned? No, sir! The next sea flung 'im with tree-mendyus force right aboard agin. That wave hit the deck like a twelve-pounder dropped from the peak. Was 'e crushed? *No, sir!* That man fell into the belly of the sail, like a babby into a feather bed. And any man wot says death wouldn't be a novelty to that man is either a liar or no gentleman."

Cookson's yarn was greeted with a laugh, which sounded louder in the cessation of the music. Ben Larkin led Grizel to a seat, and the coast-guard treated Captain Grant to a playful poke in the ribs as the young couple began what was apparently a very personal conversation.

Smuggle-erie seemed to pay no attention, but busied himself about the floor, arranging the next dance, which was that half-savage Highland romp—

Love or Duty?

the schottische. As it is properly danced in Scotland, the partners face each other, hands on hips, dance a few steps and trip off to the left, a few more steps and run to the right, then with a " Hooch ! " they fling themselves into each other's arms and swing around with such momentum that the lady invariably loses her footing.

But there was something extraordinary about this schottische. The eyes of a great number of men were upon Smuggle-erie. He suddenly looked across the room at Giles Scrymegeour, who nodded his head with a mysterious grin. The next moment the young sailor was whispering in Blind Johnny's ear. The old fiddler and his son tuned up, while the dancers got ready, all asking, as usual, what the tune was to be.

The fiddles struck up, and immediately Ben Larkin gave a start, for it was the tune that had puzzled him so often. At the same time he failed to hear Grizel's quiet voice; for close by him a gruff voice said incautiously and with a note of exuberance:

" That means the morrin's night ! Come on, lads. Kick up yer heels ! "

Next moment the floor was swarming, not only with couples, but with pairs of men, principally of the Thistle Down's crew, who romped around boisterously, humming the lively air and stamping their feet at the beginning of every line.

Although Larkin thought he perceived significance

[117]

in it all, there was to the uninitiated nothing more than the usual horse-play of the late dance, when cheeks are warm and eyes bright.

All at once Smuggle-erie's voice rang out at the beginning of a verse:

"Pease brose again, mither, pease brose again!"

And from almost every man in the room came the response in a roar of delight and enthusiasm:

"Ye feed me like a blackbird, and me yer only wean!"

"When does the Thistle Down sail?" Ben Larkin suddenly asked, turning to Grizel.

"To-morrow night," she replied innocently.

"Grizel, ye haven't given me a dance yet," said Smuggle-erie, coming up. "Is the 'admiral' to get them all?"

"Certainly, I'll dance, Smuggle-erie," replied Grizel, with a little toss of her head. "It's you that have na asked me."

The two of them danced away into the crowd leaving Ben Larkin with his heart heavy, not because she had gone off with his rival, but with a sense that he was being made a fool of—as if missiles were flying around his head from some unseen source.

He looked over the great room, and presently his eyes fell upon Captain John Grant and Giles Scrymegeour. The two men were standing apart, and, at a glance, Larkin was aware that they were engaged in a quiet, tense argument.

The big sea-master's face was as black as a storm-cloud. His mouth was set like a steel trap and his arms were folded across his breast. Scrymegeour, in order to whisper, was standing almost on tiptoe to reach the giant's ear, and the miser's ratlike face was stuck forward in an insinuating manner.

Larkin saw Grant suddenly turn upon his heel, say something decisive over his shoulder, and walk out of the hall. He did not come back.

When the wild dance was over, the smugglers—or, rather, the crew of the Thistle Down—melted away also. Smuggle-erie, alone of that brotherhood, remained in the hall. He presently brought Grizel back to her former partner, and surrendered her with a readiness that was as astonishing to Larkin as it was, somehow, disappointing to Grizel.

The nut-brown lass, it may as well be said truthfully, had not enjoyed her evening as much as the old coast-guard supposed. She had danced with the handsome young officer to the exclusion of nearly everyone except the laird. Even that social triumph had not taken from her heart a bitterness which had suddenly sprung up with regard to Smuggle-erie. She had expected that she would have humbled her daredevil lover to the dust. In her heart she had decided that, before the night was over, she would have granted Smuggle-erie the forgiveness for his former churlishness which she had fully expected he would have asked.

Smuggle-erie, however, had apparently played her at her own game. What it cost him she had no means of knowing. All she did know was that he had left her, unprotested, in the hands of his rival, and had seemingly enjoyed himself in every dance with every other lass. Before that night she had never stopped to consider which of the two lovers she preferred. Now she knew that she preferred one of them, but which?

A woman's heart, under such circumstances, is often as much of a mystery to herself as it is to her admirers. She suddenly felt a dependence on Ben Larkin, but the thought that such dependence was Hobson's choice, stung her pride. When the lieutenant requested the honor of the next dance—with a confidence that it would be granted because it was the last—she pettishly declined, and a few minutes later Ben Larkin saw her tripping with the laird.

But he captured her at the last, when the dancers were dispersing. The harvest-home itself was over, but there was something further in connection with it that Ben Larkin had in mind. Mrs. Martin, who should have been at the celebration, was confined at home with the " rheumatics," as she put it, and the girl's escort had been left to her father and the host of other lasses who would be homeward bound for Morag. Larkin, however, adroitly bore her off alone, determined to profit by his opportunity.

The short distance to the gate of the cottage with the flagstaff was passed over in significant silence. Larkin had only one thing to say, to the exclusion of all others. He would have talked out that one thing, but he felt all at once that the time was unpropitious. What he had to say had been all cut and dried in his mind, but the incident of the last dance had upset his calculations.

At the gate he took her hand, having decided that, after all, " Good-night " would be sufficient for the occasion.

The touch of her fingers sent all his ideas flying, and he could only blurt out:

" You are angry with me, Grizel? I was so happy until the—until the last. What did I do? Just tell me."

" Angry at you? " she echoed. " Why should I be angry at you? "

She impatiently tried to draw away her hand, but his closed firmly over it, and it lingered.

" I—I'm angry at myself," she said, with a queer gulp.

" Grizel! " he said, his voice deep with feeling, " until you ran off and left me like that, I felt that

between you and me there would be no need for words
—that you would know before I spoke what was in
my heart to say. I love you, lass, and if you love
me I'll go to my sleep to-night the happiest man in
Morag—the proudest man in the king's service.
Grizel——"

Her chin hung low on her bosom. He could see the
glint of her brown hair in the starlight, and hear the
soft, deep sound of her breathing. But she gave no
answer. Nor did she withdraw her hand. Even
when his arm stole around her shoulders and his hand
raised her face to his, she made no sound, nor did she
resist. It was sweet to her; and though she felt
shame, something bound her with cords of joy.

Yet there was a sting of regret. She had known
Smuggle-erie so long; and though he had hurt her, it
seemed hard, unfair, to give him up like this.

She opened her eyes, but did not look into Ben's
face. Her gaze sought the stars beyond his shoulder,
and the memory of many a communing with them
reminded her that the great moment of a woman's
life had come. She must answer—she must answer.
And by her answer would come woe or weal for him
and for her and for Smuggle-erie.

"Tell me, Grizel, is it that you love someone better?" he said. "Just tell me and I'll go. But I
think you do love me, little woman. Look at me,
Grizel—look at me and you'll know."

Love or Duty?

She slowly turned her eyes, and they lifted to his. The dim starlight fell on her upturned face, and he could see the earnestness of her gaze. It seemed years while he watched the changing thoughts in it. Hers was no love that would flash up and die as quickly, but a deep tide that moved unseen and would swell with time.

"Grizel!" he whispered.

She opened her lips as if to speak, but suddenly they hung, parted. In the stillness, to their straining senses, came voices from the cottage.

Larkin raised his eyes impatiently. The window of the parlor was open, for the night was a little sultry.

Giles Scrymegeour was speaking within.

"The ship is mine!" he said, raising his voice angrily.

Captain Grant replied:

"I'll fight ye on that. Even so, I'll not be master of it with another dishonest keg."

"Then let yer lass marry Smuggle-erie, and I'll gie ye back yer signature an' make the lad skipper."

"The lass'll not marry him on these terms!" was the sullen response.

"Weel," said the voice of Scrymegeour, after a long pause, "ye've turned gey releegious in yer auld age, but releegion was no made to save John Grant and put his freens in jail."

" I will not turn informer," said the other sullenly.

" Na? " sneered old Scryme. " It would be a bonny piece o' information that a' man wi' your record could furnish, nae doot. Ye were no that parteeklar in the past aboot yer women folk."

" I have suffered for it," was the monotone response.

" Ye micht suffer worse again if a wee bird, for instance, was to whisper in your lass's ear that her father, Captain John Grant, was Heather Bloom, wanted by the king's——"

Giles stopped, as if frightened himself by the words he was thus recklessly using.

There came a guttural, comprehending " Ah!" from Grant; then the parlor window shut suddenly, and there was silence.

Larkin's arm had never untwined from the girl's body, nor had her eyes shifted from his, but into them had come a look of dread—agony—despair.

When the Fates had wrought their worst upon her, she drew herself away from his unresisting clasp and stared unbelievingly at his pain-stricken face.

" Oh! " she whispered, and the word was drawn out like a moan. " Oh, my father! My father!"

He looked at her. His throat was choked with the sense of the great wrong she had suffered. The helplessness of his own position paralyzed him.

" Forgive me, lass! " he suddenly cried.

Love or Duty?

" It's not you—must ask," she sobbed. " Oh, my father!   My father!"   And with a weariness of pain in her voice, she turned away with a sobbed " Good-night."

" Good-night, lass," he said hoarsely.

Then, as she walked toward the cottage, he looked up at the stars, and laughed—bitterly.

CHAPTER X

THE COUNCIL IN THE CAVE

BEN LARKIN staggered back to the coast-guard station that night like a drunken man. Fate had waved a sword between him and his love. In that magic flash he had seen the impossibility of happiness with Grizel, and at the same time the blade had hewn a clear-cut path to his duty.

He was too dazed with the sudden searing of his soul, and the memory of the girl's agony, to form any plan of action. He could think only of two things —that his duty was to arrest Captain John Grant in the name of the king, and, by that act, inflict agony upon himself and upon the woman he loved.

Alas, for himself and Grizel! If he had only lingered a moment longer by the gate and taken his cue to action from what he would have seen, it might have saved a world of trouble.

He was hardly out of sight of the cottage with the flagstaff before the door opened and Giles Scrymegeour came out followed by Heather Bloom.

The miser looked carefully about to see that they

were not observed; then the two men started in the direction of the Bull Rock.

Neither spoke a word, but their footsteps went by mutual understanding of the destination. Giles walked with the nervous, light step of a man who is keyed up by past events and eager to get done with future ones. His companion strode along with his head sunk on his chest, like one who hates what he is doing, but has decided to do it.

They came to the abandoned lodge by the gate. The last of the merrymakers had straggled home, and the castle grounds were as still as on any other night of the year, when not one in a thousand of the countryside would have ventured near the " haunted " lodge.

Old Scryme gave the whistle, and, at the response, they marched up to the door of the " deserted " house, which was opened quickly to admit them.

Without any ado, Scrymegeour and Heather Bloom stepped inside, climbed down the ladder to the cave, and an unseen sentinel closed the trap-door after them.

Inside the cave, there were half a dozen smugglers sitting upon old boxes and barrels around a keg, upon which were a bottle and glasses and a tallow dip. Among the men were Smuggle-erie, Grogblossom, and the Red Mole, the latter having the appearance of intoxication. They rose to a man as Heather Bloom appeared.

" Well! " the big sea-master growled. " What's all this stage play about? What's this council for? Have none of you any understanding, or are my brains unusually sharp? As I take it, the stuff will leave Cothouse to-morrow night—or to-night, I suppose—at twelve o'clock, which will bring it here at one, or a bit later. Smuggle-erie will see it through, and the Thistle Down will sail at dawn. Is that clear enough, or must I sit here all night and drive it into you? "

Heather Bloom topped his sarcasm with a curse. The Red Mole looked sleepily across at Giles Scrymegeour, who flashed him a knowing, but nervous grin. Smuggle-erie's brows knitted, and he glanced from the king of smugglers to the miser. He saw at once that there had been a conflict.

" Aye, aye, sir! " said he soothingly. " It's all clear. But we don't want any risk about this— especially this."

" Aye, this—*especially* this! " Heather Bloom ripped out. " Men of the Thistle Down! " And he addressed them all in a comprehensive wave of his hand. " Understand what I have to say:

" You have served me, and those behind me, and yourselves, pretty well in the last twenty years. We've established for ourselves a reputation that has sent better men to the gallows. My schooner has at various times shown a creditable pair of heels to the government's craft. I personally have stood on the poop of my ship, toasted the damnation of the king, and flung the glass at the revenue officer's head.

"Very good! Very admirable! But, once and for all, that's done with. If, after to-night, the Thistle Down sails again with John Grant as master, it will be with an honest cargo and an honest crew. I'll no more see my girl dance to the tune of her father's crime." This with a savage glance at Smuggle-erie. "I'll no more yield to a worm in distorted human shape who drives me to sea on the innocence of my lass. You're a bad lot—and I've been the worst of ye—but I've always found that you were men, in spite of your failings. I put it to you as men: Would you force a man to commit a crime with the threat of babbling his former crimes to his daughter—my daughter, Grizel Grant, who thinks her father, John Grant, a pillar of respectability, while all the time he is a miserable, thieving, tax-dodger, slaving under the mortgages of that slimy eel you see there oozing with fear?"

Heather Bloom's finger pointed straight at Giles Scrymegeour, whose face was set in a sickly grin, in an attempt to pass over the matter as a jest.

The Vanishing Smuggler

The smugglers looked at the miser and growled their disgust. Smuggle-erie gave a short laugh and said:

" Suppose we tie a stone to nunky's feet and drop him in the pool, as he was for doing with me twelve years ago? "

The suggestion met with some approval. Old Scryme's grin became more sickly. Grant rapped his knuckles on a barrel-head.

" If ever I was near tempted to murder, or approve murder of, anything, it is now," he went on. " But enough of this! I've passed my word, and I'll keep it. I'll run the Thistle Down and her cargo through. But this is the last time. And if any man has anything to say, let him say it now, or forever after hold his peace! If he doesn't, he'll have the man *that was Heather Bloom* to reckon with! "

One of the smugglers got to his feet, urged by a few of the others, and saluted awkwardly.

" Sir," said he, " we're mighty sorry to lose ye— me an' the rest. Ye've been a good seaman and a better smuggler. What you said was always the word for us. An' as for anything else, we'll stan' by ye, cap'n—in spite o' him! " The speaker gave a vicious nod in the direction of Old Scryme and sat down.

The Council in the Cave

"Thanks!" said the captain shortly. "Now, then, to business!"

The bringing of the whisky from Cothouse was gone over, and the safest mode of conveying it aboard without suspicion. From the discussion, it was apparent that the Thistle Down was bound ostensibly for Bristol, but that there was a rendezvous off a lonely part of the English coast for the transfer of the illicit liquor. This also was fully gone into, as was the matter of the tides.

"The only difference this trip," said Smuggle-erie, "is the extra trouble to be expected from the revenue in the Firth. What about the coast-guard, and Mr. Horneycraft, and the officer with the brass buttons? Cookson, of course, don't count. The dominie always spends Sunday night with him, and once these two are together you could take away the coast-guard station, roof, telescope, and all, without interrupting old Jack."

"Horneycraft?" said Heather Bloom. "Remember, I can have no possibility of a trap this time. What about Horneycraft?"

There was silence, broken by Smuggle-erie.

"Where *is* Horneycraft? He hasn't been near Morag for three days. Alec was on his track. What about Horneycraft, Sandy?"

Alec, or Sandy, a young, light-haired smuggler, scratched his head and looked confused.

"I canna rightly say," he said. "For two days he was prowlin' up aroond the Red Mole's place, as the Red Mole kens."

"What about him, Red Heid?" demanded Smuggle-erie, roughly shaking the Red Mole, who had fallen into a drunken sleep.

"Eh?" said he stupidly, half waking up. "Wha? Hoarneycraft? He'll no bother ye. *He's dead!*"

"Eh!" thundered Heather Bloom. "What is that man saying?"

"Eh?" cried the Red Mole, waking up to his full senses. "What was ye sayin'? Aw—Hoarneycraft! I dinna ken. How should I ken? But he'll no bother ye. Archibald'll atten' t' that." And he fell asleep again.

Heather Bloom looked from the drunken animal to the men around the cave. His eye fell upon Giles Scrymegeour, who was grinning and wiping his lips with his handkerchief.

"You were at Cothouse to-night?"

"I was *not!*" asserted the miser.

"Eh?" muttered the Red Mole.

"Did ye murder the man?" asked Smuggle-erie at playful random.

"Murder!" gasped Giles. "Guid forgie us, what an awfu' word! I tell ye I wasna at the Cothouse masel'. But trust Archibald—trust Archibald!"

The Council in the Cave

The matter was dropped, and Lieutenant Ben Larkin was the new subject.

"There, to tell you the truth," said Heather Bloom, "is the only man I'm afeared o'. What he does not ken, I am certain he suspects. He is the man whose doings must be watched."

CHAPTER XI

SMUGGLE-ERIE FALLS FROM GRACE

WHATEVER plan Smuggle-erie had in mind for the outwitting of Ben Larkin—if, indeed, he had any—was upset next day by a curt note from Grizel Grant. It was inclosed in an envelope, and was handed to him by Daft Tommy, who was Morag's "ne'er-do-weel," save in the matter of simple errands. The note read:

> Be so good as to meet me by the castle gate after kirk service to-night. I have discovered something upon which you can further enlighten me and, besides, I feel that you and I should better understand each other before I speak to my father.
>
> GRIZEL.

"Now, I wonder if this was meant for me or somebody else?" Smuggle-erie asked himself, as he stared at the odd message and then glanced back at the slack-jawed, dull-eyed idiot who had brought it. "Who gave you this, Tommy?"

"Miss Girzie," said Daft Tommy, chuckling and grinning. "An' she gied me a bawbee an' promist to marry me—oh, aye! She promist to marry me,

[134]

an' I've got witnesses to prove it—witnesses to prove it!"

Smuggle-erie paid no attention to the lad's delusion, but frowned at the letter on his knees. He was seated on an overturned boat on the beach, and as he read the message for the fourth time he slowly nodded his head.

"Here!" said he, cutting a chew of tobacco and tossing it to Daft Tommy. "Tell Miss Girzie that you gave me the letter and that I said 'All right.'"

With many a chuckle Daft Tommy went off with the answer, and Smuggle-erie was left with the note on his knees. The thing was a mystery to him. If it had been intended for his eyes, then its contents were as Greek, although, if it was to be accepted just as it read, Smuggle-erie was sure that something had happened at the cottage with the flagstaff. It could only be that Grizel's eyes had been opened to the smuggling.

Against that was the idea that the note had been intended for Ben Larkin, and as Smuggle-erie reread the missive with this in mind he bit his lip savagely. One way or another, Larkin figured largely in it. If Grizel had discovered the secret of the smugglers, then it was time 'finis' be written to Larkin's love-making, and if it was merely that the note had been delivered into the wrong hand——

"So that's where they are!" thought Smuggle-erie.

Having accepted the mistaken delivery idea for the moment and abandoned himself to a fit of savage jealousy, Smuggle-erie's next thought was what he should do with the note. Send it to Larkin? Well, it might not be intended for Larkin. Send it back to Grizel? It would be risking an insult. Go and ask her for whom she had intended it? And if she should say "Larkin"? Smuggle-erie shrank from the humiliation. Then, with a laugh at his own stupidity, he picked up the envelope which he had thrown upon the sand. Upon it was written in a steady, schoolgirl hand: "Mr. Dick Scryme-geour."

Of course, it was for him! Then what did it mean? His conscience—the conscience of the shrewd rather than of the guilty—told him that it could be but one thing she had discovered. But how? Was it possible that Old Scryme had enlightened her a little in order to force Grant to sail the contraband to England? Or had the miserly demon done it to bring about Grizel's marriage with Smuggle-erie, so that his grip might be tightened upon all concerned? After the first flash of rage at this possibility, Smuggle-erie dismissed the idea as both unlikely and unprofitable. No! Grizel had discovered something by accident, or possibly through Larkin.

Smuggle-erie Falls from Grace

Smuggle-erie smiled. If this were so, the revenue officer had scored a point—his first—and a doubtful one at that. Smuggle-erie could play that game, too. He remembered his promise to "attend to Larkin," and now a plan began to take shape in his mind.

True, the plan was not a highly honorable one. Indeed, it was the very opposite; but Smuggle-erie would not shrink from it if he were at all sure that Ben Larkin had whispered his suspicions in the girl's ear. To his mind two wrongs could easily make a right.

He read the note again, folded it very carefully, and held it between his forefinger and thumb, the while he looked blankly across the calm Firth. He had read of the thing in a book—the thing he contemplated; he had read of it often, without believing that it could ever present itself in life as a matter easy of execution. But he never remembered having read of such favorable circumstances as presented themselves in this case. The addressing of the envelope would be an easy matter. Surely Lieutenant Ben Larkin had not progressed so far in his lovemaking that he was minutely acquainted with her handwriting. And, then, the letter itself was prefixed with no name, nor did it contain any subjectmatter that might not have been addressed to a perfect stranger. Indeed, it was the tone of it that had made Smuggle-erie think for a moment that it was not intended for him.

He sat on a boat for a half-hour, his brows knitted and his underlip stuck out. It never occurred to him that it would be dishonorable to trap Larkin with Grizel's note; but, nevertheless, he was uneasy about it. It was not his kind of fighting; that was all. He would have scorned to strike a man when down, or to hit an antagonist below the belt in a fist-fight. While his uneasiness over what he contemplated may have been really an instinctive aversion to a mean act, yet his untutored chivalry failed to understand or to concern itself with more than the probable success of the enterprise.

Finally, he shrugged his shoulders and went away toward Giles Scrymegeour's shop, where " nunky " was presently mystified by his usually boisterous " nephew's " silence and his diligent destruction of envelopes and quills. Smuggle-erie labored over that envelope address for an hour, his forehead damp with perspiration and his tongue hanging from the corner of his mouth as he toiled with the intricacies of the " i-e-u " in " lieutenant."

That it was a monument of misspent energy he would have realized had he seen Larkin, an hour or two later, tear the envelope open and cast it aside. The lieutenant glanced impatiently over the message, for he was in no good humor, but suddenly his face

The coast-guard men and the cutter would patrol
the Firth from dusk

brightened as his eyes fell upon the magic word—
" Grizel." He sat down in the coast-guard station
and puzzled long and deeply over the message.

She had discovered something upon which he could
further enlighten her—further! Of course, it was
the matter of her father. He reflected that she
might have spared him the pain of that. His position
was bad enough, and his duty was clear enough.
But she " felt " that he and she " should better understand each other " before she spoke to her father.
She could not mean love. That were preposterous
under the circumstances.

" ' You and I should better understand each other
before I speak to my father,' " he echoed mentally.
" What can she mean? It can't be that she would
have me—that she would trade with me! ' Understand each other? ' ' Understand——' The thing
is impossible, anyway! " With that he flung the
letter on the table in the coast-guard parlor and
made up his mind not to think more of it.

He would not keep the appointment. No profit
could come by it, but pain to both. His duty was
clear, although the way to it was not yet free of
obstacle. But his plan had been formed before this
message arrived.

The Thistle Down was to sail at dawn, with the
tide. The coast-guard men and the cutter would
patrol Morag and the Firth from dusk until the

schooner was out of sight. Of one thing Larkin
was certain; that the Thistle Down would sail with
every man of her crew aboard, or satisfactorily
accounted for—especially Smuggle-erie! Without
that man aboard, the schooner should not weigh
anchor. He was determined on this point. It would
be smuggling of an amazing order which could escape
the vigilance of the coast-guard this night.

So far he had not communicated his orders to Cookson or to the men. He was still waiting with im-
patience and a growing uneasiness for the reappearance of Horneycraft. Where *was* the man? He
had been missing for two days, although Larkin had
heard it rumored that he was seen around the Cothouse but twenty-four hours before. What was the
man doing? It was the thought that possibly the
long-nosed collector had discovered something which
stayed the lieutenant on the decision of a definite
plan of action. He had no desire to conflict with
Horneycraft, if it could be avoided.

He picked up the letter, and read it over and over.
He wondered what the girl could have to say. It
could be nothing against her father that she had
discovered. He knew Grizel too well to believe that
she would reveal anything against her parent,
Heather Bloom though he was. Then, what could
it be?

When six o'clock came that evening, Larkin was

impatiently walking up and down on the strip of
sand below the barren rocks where the coast-guard
station stood. The old bell of the parish kirk was
humming over the bay and echoing among the hills.
It brought back to Ben's mind the parlor of the
cottage with the flagstaff, on the previous Sunday
evening, and in his mind he presently heard the
tender passion of the little harmonium and saw the
firelight glint of Grizel's brown hair and pink cheek.

"*Meet me by the castle gate after kirk service
to-night!*"

The words echoed in his brain with the humming
of the kirk bell. He could imagine her walking
demurely through Morag at that moment with her
book of psalms and paraphrases, and presently her
voice would join with the others in praise of her
Maker. He knew now that she had been innocent
of all knowledge of the smugglers; and, knowing that,
was it not his duty to obey the order of the message?
It must be something that he *ought* to know; he
felt that, otherwise, the delicacy of the sweet lass
would have forbidden that letter.

He stopped in his walk, and in another moment
he had decided. He would go, and trust the interview to yield some guiding-point for the night's
action. It might be something about Horneycraft—
a message from Horneycraft, even. In any event it
would be but an hour's delay. During that time the

smugglers could have little chance to get away with a contraband boat, for it was still the long light of the Indian summer evenings. It would hardly be dark before nine o'clock. The cutter lay ready by the gangplank, and the crew smoked their pipes while awaiting orders in the coast-guard station.

The kirk bell stopped as Larkin retired to his room and prepared himself for the meeting with Grizel. He smiled as he remarked his own little vanity in the details of dress, and he was unashamed to admit to himself that his heart beat a higher note at the prospect of seeing her again, for weal or woe.

He took a long time to dress, so that when he left the coast-guard house, smart in his bright uniform, and stepped jauntily toward Morag on his way to the castle gate, the good folk were coming from the kirk. Toward the coast-guard station, arm-in-arm, came the dominie and old Cookson, both of them already involved in lore and history. Ben Larkin passed a few words of instruction to the coast-guard and, with a respectful salute to the dominie, passed on.

As he went through Morag, he saw, some way ahead of him, the neat little figure that had become the center of his life. She did not stop at the gate of the cottage with the flagstaff, except to cast a glance over her shoulder. Whether she saw and recognized Larkin, he had no means of knowing, but she quickened her step and walked rather hurriedly toward the castle gate.

Larkin wondered at this. Why could she not speak to him by the cottage gate? Why all this mystery? He suddenly remembered, with an uneasy qualm, that the castle gate was by the Bull Rock, the scene of his previous misadventure. He wondered if the precedent might be taken as an omen.

The coast road, as it neared the castle gate and the lodge, curved somewhat, so that Ben lost sight of Grizel until he was almost within speaking distance of her. Then, even in the dim light of dusk, he noticed an attempt on her part to conceal herself in the shadow of the broken-down estate wall. He advanced swiftly and held out his hand.

" You sent for me, Grizel? "

She drew back with a sudden, frightened widening of her eyes, which he noticed at the moment and did not fail to remember later.

" I—sent for you? " she faltered.

" Did you not? " he asked, drawing back stiffly.

" I don't understand. I—you——" she stammered.

Before he could say anything, a cloud fell across his vision and he experienced the dry, disagreeable sensation of cloth enveloping his head. Simultaneously his arms were pinioned behind him and a voice said quietly:

[143]

" Don't make a noise! Nobody means you harm."

For answer, Ben Larkin exerted all his strength
and succeeded in flinging off the grip that held his
arms pinioned. He threw his hands to his head in
an effort to get rid of the smothering cloth, but at
the first sign of a struggle he found himself in the
embrace of two or three men.

The struggle lasted less than a minute. He was
conscious, through it all, of a strangely familiar
voice, whispering:

" Don't hurt him! Don't hurt him!" Then,
when it was apparent that Larkin had no intention
of yielding, the same voice said: " Knock him on the
head, then, but—careful!"

The next moment Larkin experienced a dull shock
in the back of his neck. He fell into abysmal darkness, through which a bitter, despairing voice cried:

" Ben! Ben! Oh, forgive me! Forgive me!"

CHAPTER XII

A THOROUGH UNDERSTANDING

"Yes, sir!" cried the coast-guard, bringing down his fist with an emphatic crack on the arm of his chair. "Orders is orders, and if the adm'ral says, 'Stand by till I come alongside,' stand by it is! But where in thunder is the lad? One o'clock in the morning, sir!"

Jack Cookson glared at the old clock, whose pendulum was wagging relentlessly through the hours, and snorted with all his might and main.

"First Mister Horneycraft. Now the adm'ral. By thunder! *I'll* be missing next!"

"Indeed," said the dominie, who sat up with the coast-guard, sharing his alarm when a cessation of story-telling had reminded them that the hour was late and Larkin still absent; "indeed, is it not our duty—your duty rather—to institute a search party?"

"Sir!" snorted Cookson. "With all due respecks for book-larnin' an' sich, do you dare to tell me what my dooty is? Orders is orders, sir, and here I sit till the mornin' watch, or until the adm'ral comes

[145]

aboard. Strike my colors, sir? Do you take me for a Frenchman?"

"Orders *is* orders," said the dominie wisely. "Indeed, I do not doubt but what you may be in the right of it, my friend. England's greatest victories —leaving aside England's greatest blunders—are due to this great sense of the written rule, as applied to duty. So it was with the Romans and the Spartans. But there is no rule, my friend, which is not susceptible of exception, and something tells me that in this case your orders are in conflict with your duty. It is now six hours since Lieutenant Larkin left the station——"

"Sir!" Cookson thundered. "That may be book-larnin'—an' for book-larnin' an' sich there's none has such a mighty respeck as John Cookson, quartermaster, sir, in the service of his majesty, God bless 'im!— but the bookedest larn'dest professor in the whole country can't tell me there's a difference atween orders an' dooty."

"You misconceive me!" the dominie protested. "One's orders may, on an occasion, conflict with one's personal sense of duty. For instance——"

"What do you know of conflict?" roared Cookson. "I tell you, conflict or pipin' times o' peace, *dooty is dooty and orders is orders!*"

There came a sudden, feeble beating at the door.

"What's that?" said the dominie with a start.

A Thorough Understanding

" What's what? " the coast-guard bellowed. " Just what I say, and let it rest at that. Dooty, sir——"

Even Cookson stopped. The feeble beating at the door was suddenly reënforced by a faint voice—a woman's voice—crying:

" Mr. Cookson! Admiral Cookson! Open the door! "

A moment later Larkin staggered into the parlor of the coast-guard station alone. His uniform was covered with mud and slightly torn. His face was pale as a dead man's, but his eyes were bright with the insane glow of a disordered intellect. He swung on one heel for a moment, then lurched forward into the dominie's arms.

" Muster the men! " he gasped. " The smugglers are out! "

" Smugglers! " roared Cookson, blowing like a grampus. " You mean to tell me that they have dared to strike down a king's officer? What ho! Coast-guard! Turn out! Turn out! "

The dominie staggered under the weight of Larkin and managed to get him on the settle. The lieutenant opened his eyes and smiled up in the kind old face.

" Here I am again," he whispered. " Sunday's my unlucky day and—and—that's my unlucky place. Tell Cookson—the lodge—Bull Rock." His eyes closed and his face took on a gray-blue pallor.

" Mmmmm! " hummed the dominie. " I shall examine his skull. But, first—plenty of air—plenty of air."

Having loosened the sick man's collar, he turned and opened all the windows, through which came the ruffle of oars and the tramping of the coast-guards' feet. The dominie, in the professional preoccupation of the moment, forgot to give Cookson the instructions he had received, and only remembered them some time afterward, when Ben Larkin, opening his eyes, said:

"And find that woman—yes, find that woman! She went away!"

Two hours later, when Cookson with his men returned, empty-handed and with no information, the lieutenant was dozing under the influence of a drug the dominie had administered.

"Nothing serious," said the old-fashioned physician, smiling. "He has had a blow on the head, but I find no fracture, although sometimes the best may err on that point. He will have fever—yes, he will have fever. That, I fancy, will be the worst."

"By thunder!" stormed the coast-guard, "if ever I lay hands on the swabs, I'll keelhaul 'em an' masthead 'em and hang 'em in chains for the crows to pick!"

Larkin opened his eyes.

"Did you find the woman?" he asked.

A Thorough Understanding

"The woman?" asked the dominie. "What woman?"

Larkin sighed, and lay still for a minute or two with closed eyes.

"Grizel Grant. Her father is Heather Bloom," he said stonily. "She betrayed me—decoyed me. She brought me here."

"Oh, dear, dear!" said the dominie soothingly. "You must not talk like that. Sleep, my friend— try to sleep."

The coast-guard sorrowfully tapped his head. Larkin was, indeed, half delirious, but at intervals he so harked back to the subject that the dominie was finally moved to believe the patient was in earnest.

"Arrest the master of the Thistle Down!" said Ben Larkin faintly. "Sequester the ship——"

"But the Thistle Down's gone!" said Cookson. "I saw her weigh ten minutes ago."

The lieutenant groaned and turned a reproachful eye upon the old coast-guard.

"Cookson," said he, "if Horatio Nelson can see you now, he's blushing for his old quartermaster."

The coast-guard stared stupidly at the sick man for a moment. Then, across his face came a look of understanding, and tears sprang into his eyes.

"Adm'ral!" he said, and his voice was choked with genuine grief. "Keelhaul me f'r a lubber. Maybe old Jack Cookson's too old for sarvice—it's

[149]

nigh on twenty-five years since Trafalgar—but I—I done my b-best, adm'ral, and——"

"Spoken like a British sailor," said the patient with a smile, and wearily holding out his hand. "Forgive me, old lad. You aren't all to blame. I'm beaten, too."

"Tut! Tut!" the dominie protested. "This is nonsense. Get out of here, Cookson. You, my friend, must sleep."

"One moment," said Larkin. "Coast-guard, find that woman—find Grizel Grant—and bring her to me—here!"

"Aye, aye, sir!" said Cookson, saluting. As the poor, old, obsolete sailor went out, he dashed away a tear and said: "I believe that's all I'm good for—overhaulin' females. But," he added to himself, by way of consolation, "I've seen things in my day!"

It was nearly noon on Monday when Larkin awoke and knew that he had been outmaneuvered for the third time. The Thistle Down was gone. That was no evidence. It had been announced that she would sail on Monday morning with the tide. He had recognized none of his assailants and, although the whole thing was as clear as day, he had but one witness to it all—Grizel!

When it was discovered that he was fully conscious, the coast-guard entered the room and touched his forehead in salute. He had been waiting outside with Grizel for hours. For once he had seen the conflict of orders and duty and had kept the girl waiting until the lieutenant should have had the full benefit of his drugged slumbers.

"Come aboard, sir!" he said humbly. "I've brought Miss Grizel, sir."

"Bring her in."

Grizel presently entered. Her face was pale and drawn, and her eyes spoke of a sleepless night and great mental pain. He could not bear to look at her, and when Jack Cookson would have retired, he called the old sailor back, for he feared the interview.

"Miss Grant," he said, "where were you last night?"

"You know," she replied in a low tone.

"Did you see the smugglers?"

"You know I did."

"Could you point them out if you saw them again?"

"I could," she replied, after a moment, and with a slight weight upon the "could."

"Did you warn them after I had mustered the guard?"

"No!"

"Or cause them to be warned?"

She did not answer. He repeated the question. Then she said:

" I may have done so, unconsciously."

" After you helped me to the door of the coast-guard, you went away. Where did you go? "

" Why must I answer these questions? " she said, with a sudden toss of her head.

" By your answering them you will save me the pain of——"

" I went aboard the Thistle Down to say good-by to my father," she interrupted.

" Thank you. You see I do not suggest even that you might have gone with the purpose of warning him."

" I did not go with that in mind, nor did I——"

" That will do. I did not mean it as a question." He suddenly held out to her a folded slip of paper. " Did you write that? " he asked curiously.

She merely glanced at it.

" I wrote it," she said simply, her eyes dropping to the floor.

" At least one other person, besides yourself, knew that you wrote this? " he said, rather than asked.

She paused before answering. It was on the tip of her tongue to correct him in his examination. He had missed a point. Had she sent it him? But she kept silence, fearing in her heart for her father, rather than for Smuggle-erie. She replied to his own question.

" That was apparent, surely."

A Thorough Understanding

" Thank you," he said, dropping the paper on the floor. " That will do now, I think." His eyes met hers, full and honest, and he added: " We better understand each other now!"

He turned his face to the wall with a sigh that was almost a groan. Grizel walked out with her hands clasped tightly before her, followed by the coast-guard.

Outside she met the dominie, who looked at her with a certain wistfulness in his kind eyes. Her lips quivered before his gaze, and in another moment she was lying in his arms, sobbing like the little girl whom the old dominie had so often dandled on his knees.

CHAPTER XIII

GROGBLOSSOM'S DISCOVERY

The Thistle Down hove to amid a creaking of gear and washing of seas. Morag lay six miles astern and the dim dawn was casting gray, chilly shadows upon the surface of the Firth. A light haze hung upon all, and before it lifted there was much to be done. In the shadow of the schooner lay a squat, slate-colored boat, piled with the contraband. Smuggle-erie swung himself aboard with a nervous laugh, and cried—in a tense manner:

"Now, lads, buckle to! We've had our work this night and we're not yet at the end o' the wood. Bear a hand, m'lads! Slings ready! Heave-o and quiet, m'lads!"

The men worked like phantoms, swiftly and silently. In threes the kegs came aboard and were stowed.

Heather Bloom stood looking on from a short distance. It was not the sharp, commanding, quick-deciding Heather Bloom of other days, but a sullen gamester who had cast the dice and knew that neither his hopes nor fears would alter the result. Only once did he speak, and that as a larger keg—a half-

[154]

puncheon, in fact—came lumbering over the side and fell with a sullen thud upon the deck.

" What's that? " he asked with a snarl. " Ye'd think we were smuggling elephants to look at it. Many a dog's been choked by that kind of greed. To one side with it. You can't stow it now. Lively below, there! "

In fifteen minutes the squat craft alongside was empty and the men clambered aboard, all except the Red Mole and his surly son, Archibald. These two began to push her off, but Grant stopped them.

" Open the cock of that boat! " he commanded, " and come aboard, you men."

The Red Mole and his son looked up in astonishment. Over the gunwale they saw the dour, bearded face of the sea-master.

" Open the cock? " echoed the Red Mole, while even Archibald gave a grunt of surprise.

" Open the cock, I say! " Heather Bloom growled. " The minute this haze lifts they'll spy her from the coast-guard. Lively, now! "

" But it's my boat an' worth sax pun', if it's worth a bawbee! "

Heather Bloom's answer was characteristic of his frame of mind. He suddenly turned, lifted a keg from the deck behind and hurled it downward into the smuggler boat. The iron-ringed dead-weight missed the Red Mole's head by an inch or two and crashed into the bottom of the craft with a force that sprung her timbers.

"Now will ye obey me!" Heather Bloom raved, as the water began to bubble around the Red Mole's feet. "Come aboard! If ye'd done it at first," he added, as the two men climbed over the side, "ye might have got her back, water-logged." He whirled around upon the man at the wheel. "Up wi' your helm, Sandy! Stand by, m'lads!"

In a few minutes the Thistle Down was under way. The wind was out of west-northwest and freshening. Presently the haze was swept away and all at once the sun rose over the hills at the headwaters of the Firth, and mountain and sea were bathed in a cold, clear light.

Heather Bloom stepped to a box behind the wheel and took out a telescope, which he leveled first upon Morag and then, with a sweep, upon the land on either side of the Firth. There was nothing in sight but a few fishing smacks on the sea, and on land the world was just awaking, smoke beginning to curl from the chimneys of the villages of Inverkip, Inellan, and the farther town of Largs. A deep sigh burst from Grant's breast, but nevertheless he hailed along the deck:

"Crack on every rag, Smuggle-erie! She'll stand it as the wind holds! Come a point, Sandy—steady, lad! Steady!"

Grogblossom's Discovery

The schooner dirled away through the merry morning waters in the long reach for the Great Cumbrae Island, abeam of which Heather Bloom brought her before the wind and the Thistle Down raced like a hound for the open channel. There was now little fear of pursuit, or of danger ahead.

All through the day the schooner made good headway; Heather Bloom never left the deck until late in the evening, when the breeze dropped rapidly. Presently there was not a ripple on the Firth and one could hear the wailing of the gulls on the ghostly rock of Ailsa, some miles ahead.

Then Heather Bloom descended to the cuddy. He sat down heavily by the table and bowed his face over his clasped hands. Had any of the crew seen him at that moment, they would have been more than astonished. Heather Bloom was praying!

During the last twelve hours he had gone through an experience which his worst enemies would not have wished him to suffer. The conscience which makes a coward had stung him sufficiently; but it was not that. The suspense of the dash from Morag had tried him to the utmost; but it was not that which bowed him in misery now. Before his mind's eye, there was the picture of Grizel, whom he had thought asleep in the cottage with the flagstaff, appearing in the ghostly gloom of the deck at the moment when his eyes and ears were straining for the signal that Smuggle-erie and his men were safe and away.

In the dim light of the first dawn, her appearance, just as he turned to give the order to up anchor and away, sent a shaft of supernatural fear through his heart. What passed between them, it would be more harrowing than just to record; but when the Thistle Down weighed on the last dishonest voyage, it left behind a lass whose heart was lightened by at least a compromise, and the schooner carried away a man who had suffered the deepest degradation of a father. There was nothing now that she did not know; that was the one consolation; but what filled his heart with black rage was all that he had not known, and which she had told him.

The door of the cuddy swung open. Smuggle-erie stepped in and slammed it cheerfully behind him.

"Pop goes the weasel!" he cried, and burst into song: "With a hilly, hilly, holly——"

Heather Bloom sprang to his feet with an oath that was in strange contrast to his previous occupation.

"Stop that!" he shouted.

Smuggle-erie's song abruptly ceased, and he stared at the skipper with wide-open eyes.

"You call yourself a man?" sneered Grant.

Smuggle-erie turned pale with shock and blazing

anger. He sprang forward and brought down the flat of his hand on the table with a decisive smack.

"What d'ye mean? Take that back—quick, or——"

The two men faced each other—the lion and the tiger. Grant was the first to speak.

"You would trade my daughter to trap a man, would you?"

His words—the tone of his voice—would admit of but one charge and one answer.

Smuggle-erie had no answer.

He knew that he was guilty. The whole significance of his conduct flashed through his mind. The uneasiness which had haunted him while he contemplated the act; the vague fear which had been with him ever since he had accomplished it and had heard Grizel's cry ring out by the castle gate, as they hurried away with the inanimate form of Ben Larkin —all revealed its full meaning to him now. His tiger-like glare softened to shame, and quailed before the big sea-master's eyes. He drew back from the table and with his eyes on the floor, his hands hanging limp at his sides and his body drooping on one foot, he said after a long silence:

"I'm sorry, sir. I never thought of it that way."

"And you would marry my lass, and be a husband to her—after that!" The infinite scorn of the skipper's tone must have stung the other like a lash. But he did not betray it.

" No," said Smuggle-erie, looking up slowly, " I don't think so." His face twitched and all at once a strange glistening, like that which heralds a tear, shone in his eyes. He suddenly burst out in an anguish of passion and protest. " I know I'm not fit for the lass. I say it to you and, by God! I'm man enough to say it to her. But what d'ye expect? I *ken* nothing. I *am* nothing. A charity lad that even took the pity of a miserable old—*Scrymegeour!* Nobody ever taught me anything, but you, and I know nothing but how to cheat the customs, defy the law, and fear neither God, king, man, nor devil. Is it my fault? I'm not a man, by your way of thinking. Tell me, Heather Bloom, as a man to the lad you saved from drowning like mongrel spawn —is it my fault?—is it *my* fault? "

" I thought better of you" was Grant's reply, for the thrust had gone straight home and the accuser had weakened. His charge had rebounded upon himself.

Smuggle-erie turned away and looked at the partition. He waited for Grant to say more, but that was all he was to hear in that strain. Presently the big sea-master's hand fell upon the younger man's shoulder.

" I forgive you, lad, as I hope to be forgiven

myself," said Grant. "It has been a lesson to me, as I hope it may be an example to you. Pray God that both of us win through this time and see an end of the cursed business. Maybe the lass might forgive you, too!"

"Not her!" cried Smuggle-erie. "She's head ower heels in love wi' yon admiral. He's the better man o' the two!" he added savagely.

"In a way, maybe," Grant qualified. "He's in a better business, but," with a bit of a relieved laugh, "we'll remedy that, lad. Come!" And he rapped his knuckles on the table in cheery fashion. "We'll remedy everything, Smuggle-erie. We'll begin again. I've promised the lass."

"Ye — what?" gasped Smuggle-erie. "She kens?"

"Aye," said Grant, averting his eyes. "She kens. She owerheard us—Scrymegeour and me. The lieutenant kens, too. There's the whole hang o't."

"Good Heavens!" said Smuggle-erie, scarcely above a whisper. He hummed a few bars of "Pease Brose Again, Mither," then broke off and said: "I wish I'd known that. Now we're all in the pickle. If he can prove you Heather Bloom, he can prove everything by rule o' thumb, almost."

"I didn't say he could prove it," said Grant desperately. "As far as I can see, Grizel's his one witness of what he overheard. He'll make nothing o' her, if it comes to that."

Smuggle-erie whistled again, sitting on the table with his thumbs stuck in his belt and his legs dangling.

"Is that all he knows?" he interpolated.

"Yes, but it's enough when you consider that he was seemingly inveigled to a certain spot by Heather Bloom's lass and there knocked over the head. And when he came to, the Thistle Down was gone. Ye'll admit that there's smugglers in Morag."

"That's just the point in our favor," said Smuggle-erie quickly. "We'll admit that there's smugglers in Morag and that the man they would be likely to get rid of would be this same lieutenant, and in very much the way that you're describing. What's that got to do with the Thistle Down and Captain John Grant, bound for Bristol with an honest cargo of general merchandise and ballast? See what I mean?" concluded Smuggle-erie, raising a pair of mischievous, blue-gray eyes to the captain's face.

"But Grizel—Grizel?" said Heather Bloom impatiently.

"Safe as the kirk," said Smuggle-erie. "Aside from the fact that she'd never say a word agin her father, even if the court asked her to, yon man, Ben Larkin, is no curmudgeon like Old Scryme. I'll wager two pounds of tobacco to a half-mutchkin of whisky that he's biting his nails at this very minute, and wondering what to do with the girl now that he's got her."

" Got her? " echoed Grant, turning pale and agitated.

" Well, ye ken what I would mean," Smuggle-erie said uneasily. " I never gave it a thought, but I see now. He'd send for her and ask her, and——"

There was a silence. Each was picturing the scene of the poor girl under the rack of inquisition, divided between her loyalty, her love, and her strict truthfulness.

" One thing," said Smuggle-erie dubiously, " Larkin's a man. If it had been Horneycraft, now, I'd ha' been for putting right back into Morag."

Again there was thought-laden silence. Grant was suffering the pangs of remorse in full fury once more. To his first agony was added the thought that Grizel was bearing the brunt of everything ashore.

Smuggle-erie was having his share of wretchedness too, although his more self-interested mind concerned itself a little with wondering why Horneycraft had sprung no surprise throughout the whole business. He had been quite sure that the long-nosed collector would put in an appearance before the Thistle Down sailed. But, no! Not a sign of him. The schooner had taken aboard her honest cargo of merchandise day after day, without a single visit from the hawklike Mr. Horneycraft. It mattered nothing to Smuggle-erie now, but he could not help wondering.

As a matter of fact, Mr. Horneycraft, as if by an instinct that outlived the man himself, was at the bottom of the trap which presently yawned around the smugglers. That night the schooner made slow but steady headway down the channel and the tension aboard was relieved. Grant, however, fidgeted about the vessel all night, his heart torn between eagerness to get forward, and done with it all, and a longing to about ship and sail back to Grizel's aid.

When morning came the breeze sharpened, and the bright sunlight raised the man's spirits. Together Smuggle-erie and Heather Bloom went to the cuddy to a breakfast of porridge, tea, and bacon. Grog-blossom was cabin-boy, as well as cook, and kept traveling from the galley to the cuddy and back as fast as he could waddle, with the various dishes.

It was while he was absent from the cabin, when breakfast was all served, that Heather Bloom and Smuggle-erie were startled by a sudden horrible yell which echoed through the ship. The yell was followed by a shuffling of heavy feet, and presently Grogblossom rushed, or rather rolled, down the companion. His face was livid with horror, and he was holding his hands over his fat paunch, while he groaned and cried:

"Oh!   O-o-o-h!   Oh!   Oh!   I'm dead!   I'm

pizened! And I've got sich a horror o' the deid! Guid forgie me! I seen it! I seen it!"

Heather Bloom jumped to his feet, grappled with the fat cook, and threw him to the floor. The big sea-master fully believed that Grogblossom had developed a form of delirium which had often been prophesied for him. Grogblossom, for all his solemnity and sanctity, was quite a tippler in his quiet way. He never drank much, but he was forever taking a nip, so that if he had fallen into the slough of drunkenness all at once none would have been surprised. His habit of tasting—a common trick with cooks—had often led him into curious scrapes, but none excelled his present experience, not even that when he tasted some poison for rats which the skipper had brought aboard.

It was some time before Heather Bloom and Smuggle-erie realized that the man was quite sane, although dreadfully frightened. Then he told his story, still with his hands upon his stomach, and stopping every word or two to utter a groan.

It appeared that, feeling tired after his morning's work, and running up and down those stairs—" and he had a weak heart "—he thought maybe he would feel better if he had a little nip of spirits, brandy or something of that kind. He had none himself, nor had any of the crew. He would have waited until after the breakfast was cleared away, to ask the captain, but, as he explained to Heather Bloom, whose eyes suddenly began to twinkle, he was feeling so ill that he doubted if he would have the strength to get as far as the cuddy. His heart, etc.

There was one of the barrels which had been swung aboard the schooner from the Red Mole's boat. It was bigger than the others—a half-puncheon, in fact —and it had not been stowed. Meaning to explain to the captain later, Grogblossom said, he took the liberty of broaching the barrel. When he tried to fill a can with what he supposed was whisky, the barrel yielded only about half a pint, then the flow stopped short. Grogblossom was puzzled, but, as he explained quaintly to Heather Bloom, the quantity that he was able to draw from the barrel was enough for all immediate intents and purposes.

" Aye, aye, sir ! " he groaned. " It was for my heart. Had it since I was a lad. Done everything for't. And so I tasted the stuff. Losh, man ! Guess what it was. It was brine—salt, herrin' brine. An' it had a taste that—— Oh! O-o-o-oh ! " groaned Grogblossom, rolling over on his side and writhing in an agony of horror. " I canna tell ye. I canna put a name to't. I pulled out the spigot and—oh, cap'n, gang an' see for yersel'. Gang an' see for yersel' ! "

Heather Bloom turned and found Smuggle-erie's startled eyes full upon him. Together they read the thought in each other's mind. They turned and dashed from the cuddy, leaving Grogblossom alone with his misery.

Along the deck they ran to the spot where the half-puncheon stood, abaft the cook's galley. One glance at the little round hole where Grogblossom had been operating was enough. Through it protruded the finger of a man, the rest of whose body was inside the barrel.

CHAPTER XIV

STAND BY TO GO ABOUT

HEATHER BLOOM and Smuggle-erie were too hor-ror-stricken to do anything for a while but look at the finger, which protruded from the barrel with a kind of devilish accusation. But the brains of both men were working rapidly. In a flash of intuition each knew the name of the murdered man; made a shrewd guess at his murderers; saw the trick which had been played upon them, and realized the terrible consequences that were likely to ensue.

Yet it was no time to stand there and glare. The crew, alarmed by Grogblossom's behavior, were crowd-ing around the barrel. Heather Bloom's eyes sud-denly shot into their midst and, in a terrible, rasping voice, he said:

"All hands on deck! Where's the Red Mole? Tomlinson, go forrard and bring aft that red-headed fiend. Saunders, you go bear a hand; and you, too, Black! Bring the young whelp, too. Never mind. He's here."

Out of the corner of his eye, Heather Bloom had seen the surly Archibald leaning against the main-

mast, regarding the proceedings with a cold, unin-
terested gaze.

He came forward at the captain's command, and
stood up before him, with his long arms dangling
listlessly at his side. Not even when the three sailors
came back with the Red Mole, whose hair was
stiff with fury and fright, did the son move an
eyelash.

Heather Bloom asked no questions, but, in a voice
shaking with dark emotions, he ordered the carpenter,
Black, to bring an ax.

" Open that barrel! " he commanded.

The schooner's crew stood around in a tense, cran-
ing circle, as the ax crashed upon the barrel-head.
Once! twice! thrice!

The barrel-head splintered and cracked. The sea-
wind hummed in the rigging, and the ocean crowded
and danced around, as if eager to hear this new tale
of the sea and bury it in its bosom.

A fourth time the ax descended, and with the
handle of the weapon the carpenter levered out the
broken bits of the head. Silently the men had crept
a step forward, all except the Red Mole and his son,
and every eye, fearing to look, looked.

At first sight it was nothing but a white mass—
coarse salt; but as they stared the fog cleared from
their gaze, and the thing took shape. All that was
to be seen of it was the thin-haired head, wet with

half-dissolved salt, but the face was the face of Horneycraft!

A groan burst from every breast. They were engaged in a nefarious trade, but, as such things went, the smugglers of the Thistle Down were not bad men. And this thing was beyond human bearing. Heather Bloom was the first to recover. He turned a pair of great, blazing orbs upon the Red Mole, who suddenly dropped on his knees and wailed:

"I never did! I never did! It's Scrymegeour's work, I tell ye—Scrymegeour's work!"

The big sea-master's arm flew out, and the Red Mole dropped to the deck, felled like an ox. As the man lay there, bleeding and unconscious, Heather Bloom raised his hand to the blue heavens and staggered away, crying to Heaven for mercy! mercy! mercy!

As his back was turned, the stoic Archibald suddenly awoke with a scream and whipped out a dirk. Out went one of Smuggle-erie's legs, and the Red Mole's son plunged headlong upon his face on the white planks.

In another moment half the crew was on top of him, beating him into insensibility. Smuggle-erie drew off and cast a glance about him. The schooner had come in the wind's eye, and the helmsman had abandoned the wheel, which was spinning idly in accord with the flapping, fluttering sails.

Stand by to Go About

The schooner's master and crew were demoralized. The young smuggler saw the breach into which he must step. He flung himself upon the mass which was struggling over Archibald, and beat the men with his fists, the while he shouted to them by name, commanding them to cease. Presently the mass broke, and the men stood up before Smuggle-erie. Archibald remained motionless upon the deck.

Smuggle-erie glared at the crew for a moment; then, rushing upon the man, Tomlinson, he drove him back to the wheel. In a few minutes he held the deck under control, and the men, their terrors renewed, as they calmly reviewed what had happened, were ready to obey an order that might save them.

"I'm going below for a minute," said Smuggle-erie sternly. "If I hear a pin drop while I'm there, I'll come up and stave in some more heads. Here, you—Black. As you're so lively wi' the ax, cooper up that barrel the way you found it. Leave these things," he added, indicating the Red Mole and his son. With that Smuggle-erie marched to the companion.

The minute he was out of sight of the crew his nerve deserted him completely, and he dashed into the cuddy with a face the color of dirty snow.

Heather Bloom was sitting on the settle, leaning heavily upon one arm. The other was flung wide and aimlessly across the table, with the fist shut so tight that the knuckles gleamed white through the brown hair of it. His jaw was fallen, and he was for all the world like a man in a cataleptic trance.

Smuggle-erie was muttering wildly and unintelligibly. The big sea-master awoke with a start, and, at the same time, he found his tongue in a burst of fury, which sounded like the raving of a wounded lion. He cursed until his breath gave out and his face turned purple; then he broke out in a hoarse peal of laughter, which ended in a wailing appeal for mercy.

Smuggle-erie watched him, at first in astonishment, then in fear that the skipper's mind had become overturned. Finally he went up to him, struck the giant in the chest, and ripped out:

"So you call yourself a man!"

The echo of another scene, it struck Grant in a peculiar manner. He stopped short, stared at Smuggle-erie, then sank down by the table with his head in his hands. To Smuggle-erie's ears came his voice, muffled and hoarse:

"Murder! Murder on my ship! She told me! She told me it would come to that! Poor little lass! If it wasna for Grizel——" He suddenly looked up, dashed his hand across his eyes, and the steel trap shut upon his face.

"What's to be done?" he snapped.

Stand by to Go About

"It's mostly done already," said Smuggle-erie coolly. "If you can find anything else to do, you've more brains than me."

"Let's take this from the beginning," said Grant, becoming strangely calm. "Horneycraft is found dead on my ship in a barrel of coarse salt. That barrel of coarse salt came from Cothouse, where Horneycraft had been prowling about looking for evidence. The Red Mole owns that place, and is responsible for every barrel of contraband aboard—he and Scrymegeour. He—Smuggle-erie!" he cried, breaking off short. "You remember in the cave, Saturday night, how this man Red Mole blurted out that Horneycraft was 'dead,' then swore he had never seen him, and how Scrymegeour said Archibald would take care of Horneycraft. Oh, why talk! They killed him, put him in a barrel, and shipped it along with the kegs. In fine, they knew that if we landed that barrel without discovering its contents, and somebody else found the body, it would be traced back to us, and it would go hard and certain with a poor devil of a smuggler because it happened to be a revenue officer who was killed. Oh, the arch-fiend!"

Smuggle-erie began to whistle.

"Why land the barrel at all?" he said after a bit. "It's customary, isn't it, to give a man decent burial at sea, even if he happens to be a revenue officer?"

[173]

"That's the dirty work he'd like to have us do!" groaned Heather Bloom.

"It's to save our necks," was the very practical retort. "We might 'bout ship and sail into Morag, but who's to take the word of Heather Bloom against Old Scryme's, in the matter of a revenue collector murdered and found dead in a barrel aboard that same Heather Bloom's ship?"

"Anything, lad!" groaned the sea-master. "I can't think—I can't think! My brain's afire and tumbling like the sea. You do it—do the best for me, lad!" And the big skipper flung out his hands in a helpless appeal to his young mate.

"Aye, aye, sir!" said Smuggle-erie respectfully. "Then bury it is. I'll make the arrangements and call you, sir. Ye might read a bit prayer afore we tilt the thing into the sea. A thing like that'll go well with a jury of land-lubbers. For the rest, skipper, don't take on hard about it. You'll have the whip hand of Giles Scryme for all time, even if you do have to explain in the end why you kept your mouth shut so long."

"It's not that, lad," said Heather Bloom; "it's the hard luck o' it. The last trip. Think o' it! The last trip! I know now that I could have been happy again; but, after this—no!—never! It'll haunt me—*haunt me, I tell you!*" And the broken man's voice arose in an agonized crescendo.

Stand by to Go About

Smuggle-erie went back to the deck. The carpenter, Black, had finished coopering up the barrel, and stood by the grewsome thing, ax in hand, like a headsman by the block upon which they were all to be executed. Tomlinson, with blood streaming from a cut over his left eye, stood sullenly by the wheel. The Red Mole still lay where he had fallen, but his son had partly recovered consciousness and had crawled into the scupper, where he lay muttering to himself.

Smuggle-erie passed Archibald and knelt down by the Red Mole's side. After a few minutes' examination, he rose with a chuckle.

" Not dead! " he said aloud. " Here, Saunders and Alec, carry him below and tie him up. You can do the same with the dummy one, there. We may need them before we're out of this wood. You, Black, rig up some sort of funeral. We're going to roll the collector overboard."

" Aye, aye, sir! " said Black, who forthwith set to work.

In about half an hour all was ready, and the barrel-coffin of the late Mr. Horneycraft stood ready by the gangway. Each of the sailors had put on his shore-going togs, and many of them came into the solemn ring with their Bible in hand. Heads bowed, they stood in a semicircle and awaited the arrival of the master. The carpenter stationed himself by the barrel, ready to knock away the wedges and to let the queer coffin roll into the sea.

When all was ready, Smuggle-erie went to notify Heather Bloom. The big sea-master was sitting just where he had left him, but at Smuggle-erie's word he rose and took a Bible from a locker under the settle. Then he slowly ascended the companion and walked toward the solemn semicircle. Several of the men looked up and nudged one another as he approached, for the captain was a strangely altered man. He seemed to have aged ten years in as many hours; but the events of the last hour had driven all the luster from his skin, and the gray of his hair showed almost white around the temples. He walked, too, with an unsteady gait, and his eyes gazed straight and stupidly before him. In silence he took his place beside the barrel. He began to rustle the leaves of the Bible and turn them idly. Smuggle-erie looked over his shoulder, with the intention of offering a suggestion, perhaps. He noticed that the captain's Bible was upside down. He was about to speak when Heather Bloom's voice—dull and distant—began the prayer:

"*Our Father which art in Heaven——*"

He stopped. The men looked up at him and shuffled uneasily. Heather Bloom's eyes were fixed upon the far seas, and he was swaying.

Stand by to Go About

"*Our Father——*" He stopped again. Smuggle-erie stepped to his side. The captain was swallowing hard, and his eyelids were flickering rapidly.

"*Our Father——*" Then, all at once, the big sea-master tottered, and he fell back into the arms of his men. Smuggle-erie gave one glance at his face. It was dark in hue, and the veins were standing out like cords.

"Bear a hand, lads!" he cried. "The devil's on this ship!"

They carried the skipper below, and several of the sailors set to work to loosen his clothes and get him into his bunk. Smuggle-erie stood by and helplessly looked on. Presently, as the captain's writhings awoke a similar commotion in his own heart, he rushed to the deck with his fists clenched and face working in fury. The carpenter was knocking the wedges from under the barrel, after a discussion with those who had remained on deck.

"Avast there!" Smuggle-erie roared. "Back with that barrel! We'll save it to save ourselves. *Stand by to go about!*"

He leaped to the wheel and jammed it down. The men sprang to their posts, too dazed to notice anything strange about the command; and as the Thistle Down swung around and filled away on a literal home-tack, Smuggle-erie, his eyes ablaze with the joy of battle, shook his fist at the north.

"You, too, old shrimp!" he cried. "Stand by to go about!"

CHAPTER XV

It was twenty-four hours after the Thistle Down
sailed before Lieutenant Ben Larkin was able to
go about his business. Indeed, if the dominie had
been asked about the matter, he would have said
that on the Tuesday morning when Ben left the
coast-guard station, the man was not fit to be out
of bed. But Ben did not ask the dominie's opinion.
" He took French leave, by thunder ! " as Cookson
said.

After Grizel left on Monday afternoon, and all
that night, Larkin lay writhing under the sting of
defeat. Defeat it was, undoubtedly. What did it
matter that he knew who Heather Bloom was, and
that Giles Scrymegeour was the mainspring of the
smugglers, and that practically the entire male population of Morag was privy to the contraband tribe?
He could prove none of it, except by Grizel, if Grizel
would speak. Something in him revolted against
employing her against anyone, when the evidence
which she could give had been got while she lay in

the arms of the man who was swearing by all the gods to love, honor, and protect her.

There was only one thing for Ben Larkin to do—get out and snare the game for himself, and in some other way. He could not do it as long as he lay in bed, but he had a clew which was legitimately his, and which he could act upon without a clash between love and duty.

That clew was throbbing in the back of his skull when he left the coast-guard station and walked away toward the castle gate. What Grizel had to do with that assault he did not know, and did not care to think. In fact, he had decided not to think any more about Grizel—any more than he could help. He would forget that she existed; at least, he would try to forget that she had anything to do with the smugglers, and even that she was Heather Bloom's daughter.

He would arrest Heather Bloom, regardless of his daughter; he would jail Smuggle-erie, in spite of the ethics of rivalry; he would turn Morag inside out and upside down, for all his love mattered!

From which train of thinking it may be suspected that Ben Larkin's brain was in a peculiarly excited condition. And no wonder. He was the hero of this business, but, unfortunately for him, he was a hero of human mold, and was not used to knocks on the head and drowning, as a regular thing. Between his escape from the sea and his latest adventure, he was in an ill condition. And it was that very feverishness of intellect which sent him, like a drink-fired idiot, upon his present mission.

He first went to the castle gate, where he had been knocked on the head. Here he had once been miraculously saved by Smuggle-erie. Here, also, by the Bull Rock, the smuggler's boat had vanished a little over a week before; and here, finally, he had once heard the mystic signal of "Pease Brose Again, Mither!" Here was the place to begin his independent investigation.

He went straight into the gardener's lodge and began a search. His fevered brain was strangely acute and imaginative. If this was a haunted place, the ghosts, he reflected, wore hob-nailed boots, the impressions of which he could see everywhere on the muddy, rotten floor. In a few minutes he found the trap-door and, with an exulting heart, descended the ladder. A cave! Exactly! And the low tide revealed a bit of sunlight at the other end.

So this was how he had been saved? He looked around the cave. There was not a scrap of anything to signify that smugglers had ever been there; but the hob-nailed imprints upstairs, the ladder, the outlet into the Bull Rock passage, all combined to satisfy him. He returned to the lodge and paused by the door. He filled his pipe and lighted it, while he carefully eyed the ground outside.

" They took no pains to hide anything," he mused, gazing interestedly upon deep wheel-marks and hoof-prints, which told how the vehicle had lingered for some time at this door. " That's the trouble about this business," he reflected; " you must catch them with the contraband in their possession. However——"

Puffing his pipe amiably, he started off on the trail of the cart-tracks. They led, not into the public highway, but through the grounds of the castle. Larkin reflected that this was an odd circumstance, but it became more interesting than odd when the tracks skirted the old castle and came out on the mountain highway at a near gate.

" A short cut," said Larkin to himself. " Somebody in the castle in the game, too. I shouldn't be at all surprised if the laird himself is in it."

Although more than twenty-four hours had passed since that cart came down the hill road, the tracks were almost undisturbed, so rare was traffic; and there had been no rain. Larkin could easily trace them, besides, by the fact that one of the wheels had sunk deeper in the mud than the other—showing that the cart had been badly trimmed. The second wheel had a distinguishing characteristic, also. It had been patched on the iron circumference, and

[182]

had left its stamp on the road every five or six yards.

Smiling at the simplicity of it all, Larkin walked on, puffing away at his pipe, until he came to Cothouse. Mrs. Currie was scrubbing the floor of the bar, the air of which was heavy with the odor of stale tobacco, bad whisky, and vinegar.

" Tell me," said Larkin in friendly fashion, " how many kegs went down on Sunday night in the cart? "

Mrs. Currie struggled to her feet, the exertion causing her fat face to turn red and damp, while her breath came in asthmatic, vinegary wheezes.

" Coward! " she gasped indignantly. " To come here with your insultin' questions to a lone, defenseless woman! "

" Your pardon, madam," said Larkin, completely taken aback, but highly amused, nevertheless. " I wouldn't insult you for the world."

" Ye'd better not! " said Mrs. Baldy Currie, regaining her breath and her barmaid manners. " I'd claw every hair out of your head! "

" I quite believe it," said Larkin. " On second thought, I'll be more discreet than valorous, madam, and retire."

So saying, he removed his hat politely and departed, leaving Mrs. Baldy Currie completely stupefied.

"He's daft!" was her final and complete estimate of Lieutenant Ben Larkin.

Larkin was not daft, by any means, but his head was whirling as if he had been drinking. The fever of his wound grew worse under his excitement, and he walked back to Morag, a thousand possibilities racing through his brain. As he was passing the rear gate of the castle grounds, it occurred to him that it would be amusing to call upon the laird and ask him about the carts.

The laird received him quite graciously. Richard Halliday was a big, stout man, with the approved bearing of a country squire. He could rip out a "By George! Egad, sir" and a "Country's going to the devil, sir!" like one to the manner born, which, it is to be presumed, he was. He also had gout, and a way of puffing out his cheeks when he was listening to anyone.

"I merely wished to ask you a few questions," said Larkin.

"Questions? Questions?" sputtered the laird. "Certainly, sir! With the greatest of pleasure, sir! An honor, I assure you!"

"You are aware, I presume, that the amount of smuggling which has been going on around here of late has——"

"Around here? Around where? Smuggling? Why, yes, of course! An outrage, sir—a damned outrage! A sign of the times we live in, and this confounded Toryism! *Smugglers*, you were saying? "

" Smuggling—yes," said Larkin with a silly laugh. " I said smuggling. The smugglers, you know "—and the laird looked astonished as Larkin gave him a friendly poke in the ribs—" the smugglers, I was saying, actually drove a cart-load of contraband whisky under the castle windows on Sunday night."

The laird staggered back a couple of paces. Larkin could not help noticing the blank astonishment on his face.

" What did you say? " he stammered, all his gruff heartiness vanishing. But it returned in a sudden way that made Ben suspect half of it was assumed. " Passed under the castle windows—under *my* windows, sir? An outrage, sir—a cursed outrage! Incredible. I cannot, I will not, believe such an assertion, sir. Under *my* windows? Why, good gracious, man! Have a glass of port? No? Oh, come, come! Oh, very well. I will not press you. A rule of mine. You were saying——"

" Saying? " echoed Larkin stupidly. " Oh, yes. The smugglers, you know."

" Hang me, sir! " cried the laird. " I wish you wouldn't *laugh* like that."

" Does my laugh annoy you? " asked Larkin quizzically.

"Yes, sir! No, sir! What the devil am I saying, anyway? You were saying——"

"I was," said Ben.

At this peculiar rejoinder the laird collapsed altogether, and faced Larkin. The lieutenant, half-crazed with fever as he was, realized that it was time he said something to obviate his being escorted to the door.

"I was speaking of the cart-load of contraband from Cothouse," said Larkin.

"Eh!" cried the laird, startled.

"And which," continued Larkin steadily, "having passed under the castle windows, one might say, and having been smuggled through a gardener's lodge on this estate, would naturally arouse the suspicion that someone in this castle was an accomplice of the smugglers."

"Eh?" gasped the laird. "Great Heavens!" And the exclamation was no squirely bluster, but a genuine explosion of fear, or astonishment. By a mighty effort, the man managed to regain his portly rôle, and blurted out: "What the devil d'ye mean, sir? How *dare* you, sir, poke *me* in the ribs! What d'ye take me for—a fishmonger?"

"You misunderstand me, sir," said Larkin quietly. "It is quite possible that one of your servants, unknown to you——"

"Ah!" cried the laird, his face clearing. "That's

more like it. That's more like it. Pardon my temper. As a child I was hasty. Positively an affliction, sir—an affliction! Have a glass of port?"

"No, thank you, sir," said Larkin. "I must be going. But keep your eyes open, laird. Keep your eyes open."

"I will, sir—I will," said the laird, a little dubious of Larkin's meaning. "I appreciate your kindness, sir. Smugglery? Huh! Let me lay hands on the rascals, sir, and I'll have them put in the stocks, sir—put in the stocks, as they used to do. Old-fashioned ways are the best, sir—old-fashioned ways, I tell ye. But there—it's the times we live in!"

And in this way the laird conducted Larkin to the front door. As he walked off, the laird saw the lieutenant's shoulders quaking, and was seized with a sudden dread. He rushed to his study, rang a bell furiously, and, when the butler appeared, said:

"Dress yourself, James. At once! You must take a letter—at once!"

Larkin, in the meantime, was proceeding on his career of temporary madness, chuckling to himself.

"The laird, too! Ha, ha! The laird, too!"

Passing the cottage with the flagstaff, he nearly ran into Grizel.

"Aha!" he cried pleasantly. "Miss Grizel. The top of the morning to you—afternoon—evening, I mean. One hardly notices the flight of time, as I was just saying to the laird."

She stopped, looked at him, and gave a start. She firmly believed for a moment that he was under the influence of liquor. Then she saw that he was ill, and a great wave of maternal pity crossed her face.

"Oh, you should not be out!" she said. "Go home, will you, please? Go home, and I will get the dominie to come and see you."

"No, madam," said he, with exaggerated politeness. "Even the pleasure of your loving kindness I must forego. You cannot tell how much it will grieve me to arrest your father and the young man; but my duty, madam, my duty!"

And, with his head erect, he marched away, after a dignified salute, leaving the girl in tears. Passing Giles's shop, the imp of mischief again seized him, and he marched inside.

"Good-morning, Mr. Criminis!" cried Larkin. "I mean to say—Mr. Scrymegeour. I was thinking of *particeps criminis*, although, after all, the name might apply—does apply, come to think of it. Good!" And the fever-crazed man laughed lightly. "*Particeps Criminis, Esquire.* Not bad! Not bad!"

And he walked right out, leaving Giles staring blankly after him and muttering: "*Particeps*

criminis! Particeps criminis! What does he mean?
What's a *particeps criminis*—eh? "

When Larkin arrived at the coast-guard station,
he found the dominie and Jack Cookson awaiting him,
both in a pretty state of anxiety.

Ben promptly poured forth his tale. It was a
remarkably accurate estimate of the whole situation,
considering that much of it was guesswork, and the
whole related by a delirious man. Horneycraft, he
was certain, had been knocked in the head. So had
he been, for that matter. That, to his disordered
brain, was quite sufficient proof.

" But the laird a smuggler! " cried Larkin boisterously, as Cookson helped him off with his boots, while
the dominie mixed a hot potion. " The laird a smuggler! That's the funniest thing of all. Well, well,
well! "

They got him to bed, finally, and induced him to
sleep, but only after he had " explained " everything
in detail, and assured Cookson that all that was necessary was to arrest Heather Bloom, Smuggle-erie, and
the whole crew of them the moment the Thistle Down
turned up. Then somebody would undoubtedly turn
king's evidence.

The Thistle Down had just left, practically speaking, and was not expected to return for a week.
Therefore, the surprise next morning was superlative,
when Jack Cookson, who had been standing on the

barren rocks reconnoitering the Firth with his telescope, suddenly burst into the sick-room and reported:

" The Thistle Down, sir! Bearing up the Firth under every stick and stitch, by thunder!"

CHAPTER XVI

QUEER DOINGS

JACK COOKSON and the men of the coast-guard were not the only persons who were thunderstruck that Wednesday morning by the sudden, unlooked-for, and unaccountable reappearance of the Thistle Down.

All Morag was set by the ears, as the saying is. All Morag knew by what sort of trade the schooner profited, and this daring return in broad daylight, in the face of the coast-guard, and, as was to be presumed, with half a hundred kegs of illicit whisky in her hold, was beyond comprehension. In fifteen minutes the whisper had run from house to house that something had gone wrong, and in twenty minutes the beach was crowded with the anxious and the curious.

But there were three persons, besides Cookson and Larkin, who were stunned with astonishment and fear. The first and second were Giles Scrymegeour and the laird. The letter which Richard Halliday had dashed off, after Ben Larkin's visit, was to the miser, warning him that " all was lost." Giles, full of dread, had taken the first opportunity, after Morag was asleep, to slip up to the castle.

Nobody ever dreamed that Laird Halliday was aware of the existence of Giles Scrymegeour even, but such is the way of the world. As a matter of fact, the laird's honor, like that of many a better man, was on paper, and reposed with other similar documents in the famous iron box. Subsequent events, which have little to do with this story, proved that the laird and his estate were mortgaged to the throat, and in the clutches of Giles.

"I tell you the game's up!" stormed the laird. "I was a fool ever to go into it. But, thank God, I've had little hand in cooking this mess."

"Except to shut your eyes," sneered Giles, "an' to lend us the cover of your guid name and an estate road."

"Well, that's nothing. What if I denied it?"

"Ye had yer share, had ye no? An' there's them as kens it. But, hoot toot! It's no as bad's that. We could prove mair agin *you* than this lufftenant could prove agin *us*. What if he does ken the stuff came frae Cothouse? There's nothing there to prove it—not even a still. We foresaw that. It's juist a clearin'-hoose for the mountain men. And what if he kens o' the cave? If there's anything there— well, Smuggle-erie's a bigger fool than I tak' him to be. I tell ye, a's safe, if we keep cool an' no meet trouble half-way. The Thistle Down's gone. Catch her if ye can, ses I! An' she'll no come back wi' anything contraband. Uncle Giles'll see to that!"

"I hope so! I hope so!" quavered the laird. "But I don't like it. See here! As you're so cocksure, I'll off to Edinburgh for a month an'——"

"Aye, aye!" said Giles coolly. "You'll off to Edinburgh, an' see the ladies, an' spen' money at the clubs an' the ilk, while old Giles, that owns the clo'es on yer very back, 's to stay at hame an' bear a' yer troubles. Na, na! Share an' share alike. That's fair do! And it cuts both ways, Mr. Halliday. But far be it frae me to remind you o' yer debts. It's no generous. We're makin' a fash aboot nothing. The man's been drunk for twa days, and he's just blethering. Why, man, it was just yesterday he cam' into my shop an' begins some haverin' aboot me bein' a—a —what d'ye call it?—a *particeps criminis!* The man's dr——"

"A what?" howled the laird. "He called you a what?"

And when Giles, with sudden fear, repeated the words, the laird turned very pale, and swore by the nine gods that he was going to Edinburgh. Then, when Old Scryme had the bit of Latin translated for him, he, too, flew into a miserable funk, and the pair of worthies sat down and considered themselves fit objects for the world's sympathy.

The Vanishing Smuggler

Giles could have argued around any definite point in the business, but this significant phrase completely bowled him over. Latin was a thing for which Old Scryme had a fearful respect, knowing none of it himself. It was the kind of language doctors wrote when they didn't want patients to know what they were giving them, and it was the kind of language Giles had seen on tombstones and heard in courts of justice. The laird, himself, was not strong on Latin, and his offhand interpretation increased Giles's fears. This was like stabbing a man in the dark.

They sat there by the big fire and argued over every possibility in the whole business. When both of them had talked themselves to despair, the laird produced a bottle of old port. Forthwith they waxed cunning, eloquent, and shrewdly argumentative, so that by the time the cocks began to crow they were agreed that all was not lost yet. Maybe that was all the Latin Larkin knew. Anyway, the best policy was to stand by and wait developments.

But when it came time for Giles to scurry back to his hole like a highly respectable rat, and the laird lifted the blind of the castle window to see that the road was clear, both of them presented gray faces toward each other, for there she was—the Thistle Down! And while the laird crammed his clothes into a grip-sack, Old Scryme scurried back to his shop,

[194]

locked the door on the inside, and sat on the iron box, all a-shake with apprehension.

Grizel was the third person who opened her eyes in wonder and terror when the schooner reappeared. She had slept little during the two nights since her father's departure. Her heart and mind were in conflict over several matters. She was happy in the knowledge that, after this voyage, Captain John Grant would never go to sea again; but, in gaining that compromise, she had grown from a child to a woman. Her happiness in the fact that she had saved her father's honor was mingled with the pain of her other love.

She could not hate Smuggle-erie for what he had done, for she believed that he had seized Ben Larkin in order that this last trip might not end in disaster. Yet her own presence and involuntary part in that business had widened the gulf between her and Ben Larkin. She made no secret of it to herself. Her heart was his, although she could never hope that his heart would be hers.

She had risen early from a sleepless bed that Wednesday morning. The first thing that her eyes fell upon was the schooner, with its curved, billowing sails. She stood stock-still in the doorway of the cottage and stared.

Then her heart began to beat like a hammer. Why were they coming back? They could not have got rid of that compromising cargo so soon. Were they mad? They surely must know what had happened before they sailed. Her father knew of Larkin's discovery, and for her sake, at least, he would never have come back into the lion's jaws like this. Then a fearful terror assailed her. Perhaps he was dead, and the others did not know all that she had told him.

Whatever the cause of the return, there was the Thistle Down. And there was the revenue cutter racing out to meet her. In the stern sat a familiar figure, Ben Larkin. Even in that moment of anguish, her maternal solicitude inwardly chafed, that he should be endangering his life again, when only the night before the dominie had told her that he was a very ill man.

But, mystery of all mysteries! What was this her eyes beheld? The Thistle Down had suddenly hove to. They were lowering a boat and into it a barrel. She could not see her father anywhere, but could clearly discern Smuggle-erie directing movements. Now she could see him lowering himself into the boat and sitting at the stern. The boat pushed off, and they were rowing toward the Bull Rock, under the eyes of the whole coast-guard, and pursued by the revenue cutter!

Grizel stared like one stricken with a hallucination. But it was true. Then they could not know that the game was up; that, whether they reached the cave or

not, the lieutenant would arrest them all. Her
father! She had never a thought for Smuggle-erie;
but, for her father's sake, she must save them all,
warn them all!

She seized her bonnet, but paused as she tied it on.
If she warned them, whether she succeeded in saving
them or not, again would she stand before the man
she loved, afraid to explain, unable to defend herself.
For a moment her mind and her heart battled. No!
Her father was her father, after all. She had always
had him, and might always have him. Larkin was
nothing to her—at least—— She tied the strings of
her bonnet, ran out of the house, and away toward the
gardener's lodge.

After all, if Ben Larkin had his duty to perform
before his love, so had she!

In the meantime, all Morag was on the beach, with
the exception, perhaps, of Giles Scrymegeour. And
all Morag was staggered at what was going on before
their eyes. They saw the cutter racing to meet the
schooner, and the men of the schooner lowering a big
half-puncheon. Why all this business about a single
barrel, when there should be half a hundred telltale
kegs still aboard? The same thought occurred to
Ben Larkin, who sat at the tiller of the cutter, crying
in a crazy voice to his men to make greater speed.

But when the boat pushed off from the schooner's
side and darted away toward the Bull Rock, he cried

a halt, for this was beyond him. Was it a trick to divert attention from the schooner? Or was the whole thing a delusion of his delirious brain? Was it possible that the fools were going to run the Bull Rock passage in broad daylight, with the tide *low?*

"Away!" he yelled, and swung the tiller to port.

The Thistle Down was too big a business to escape detection, should smuggling be tried. Besides, the boat could be captured before it reached the rock and towed back to the schooner. The men bent their backs and strained their muscles over the oars. It was the great race over again; but this time, under what altered circumstances! Larkin knew the passage nearly as well as they did. And it was broad daylight. The whole of Morag was shouting and cheering on the shore.

Bit by bit, the cutter overhauled the smuggler. The big barrel towered above the heads of the rowers, but Larkin could see Smuggle-erie over the top of it, with a grin on his face as marked as a new moon. What was he grinning about? Larkin's fevered blood boiled. He felt his very brain take fire.

His eyes saw red, and he heard himself yelling at his crew, while to his ears came the distant roar of the onlookers, who waved their arms and yelled from the very water's edge. The remainder of the Thistle Down's crew had climbed into the rigging, and they, too, were adding their lung power to the general pandemonium.

"This is madness—madness!" muttered Larkin. Nevertheless, he urged on his men.

Foot by foot they overhauled the smuggler's craft. The turn of the rock came. The Thistle Down's boat shot into the passage and was lost to sight for a moment.

"Go on! Go on!" yelled Larkin. "If he can do it, I can!"

The cutter raced into the dangerous passage, Larkin steering with consummate skill amid the grazing fangs of rock. The ripples of the smugglers' track were his only chart and compass, but on the cutter went, unharmed. Midway, the lieutenant raised his eyes. There was the mouth of the cave, yawning wide open as he had expected to find it, but——

The smugglers' track did not go near it. The ripples continued right on through the passage; and when Larkin looked, there was Smuggle-erie standing up in the stern of the Thistle Down's boat as it shot out at *the other end* of the passage.

Larkin was balked! But he had been hard to beat. The smugglers knew it. They had seen few men, least of all a stranger, dare that passage of the Bull Rock. Smuggle-erie, filled with generous admiration, took off his hat and yelled:

"Three cheers for the revenue chiel!"

The smugglers took it up, and the cheering was echoed ashore and from the rigging of the schooner.

Larkin stood up, swaying as he did so, and acknowledged the cheers of the generous victor with a salute. But in that instant he noticed that the barrel was no longer in the smugglers' boat. Where was it? He sat down quickly and yelled a command to his men. The cutter swung to the left.

"Now, m'lads!" shouted Larkin. "Two good strokes and ship oars!"

The men obeyed. With his head bent forward and his hand gripping the tiller, Larkin drove the boat right into the gloom of the sea cave. Here, undoubtedly, he would find the barrel and the smugglers' accomplices. They, at least, would be trapped, for the gardener's lodge was surrounded, if Jack Cookson had carried out his orders.

Ben Larkin was first to scramble up on the rocks. A dim shadow leaped forward to meet him. A light hand fell upon his arm, and a voice whispered:

"Smuggle-erie!"

It was Grizel. There was not another living thing in the cave, nor any sign of a barrel or smugglery. A sudden darkness swept over Ben Larkin's heart, soul, and brain.

He turned away from the girl.

"No, madam," said he brokenly. "Not Smuggle-erie. Only Ben Larkin!"

CHAPTER XVII

A SEARCH of the Thistle Down followed. Nothing came to light but the sickness of Captain Grant, who was presently carried ashore on a stretcher. Lieutenant Ben Larkin, also, was practically carried to the coast-guard station. He was completely used up.

Not a drop of illicit whisky—not a bit of contraband—had been found on the schooner. The barrel—the mysterious barrel—had vanished. Smuggle-erie's wit had completely tricked the revenue officers.

It was then that Morag heaved a sigh of relief, although the continuing topic of the day was the barrel. What was in this barrel, that so much fuss had been made about it? And where was the barrel? That was the main thing. It presently became almost a joke, and the Morag worthies chuckled on the street and along the beach, and cried jocularly to one another:

"Barrel—barrel—who's got the barrel? "

None but Smuggle-erie knew, or was at liberty to say. Grogblossom and the rest were asked, but they only shrugged their shoulders, looked preternaturally glum, and said: " Ask Smuggle-erie." That young man swaggered down the one and only street of Morag with a peculiar grin upon his face. To all questions he merely answered:

" Wait!"

Jack Cookson held a stormy interview with him, and charged him outright with being a smuggler.

" Don't answer!" he cried. " Don't you *dare* to answer! I don't need to be told. I know it, by thunder! And so does everybody."

" I wish I could help you to prove it," retorted Smuggle-erie.

" Prove it? Prove it? *Hang* proof!" Cookson bellowed. " What did you do with that barrel, ye rapscallion? "

" What barrel? " Smuggle-erie asked in mild surprise.

" The barrel I seen you put in the boat and row around the Bull Rock."

" Did you see a barrel? " Smuggle-erie inquired earnestly.

" Yes, sir—a barrel—a b-r-a-l! Ain't that plain enough? "

" A barrel!" said Smuggle-erie, pretending extreme amazement. " Here!" he added, angrily turning upon the grinning crowd. " Who's got that barrel? "

"*Barrel—Barrel—Who's Got the Barrel?*"

Whereat the crowd burst out in a roar of laughter. Joining hands, they danced in a circle around the coast guard, sing-songing like children:

"Barrel! Barrel! Who's got the barrel?"

The coast-guard, fuming with rage, stamped away, after cracking several over the head with his ancient telescope. Smuggle-erie, himself, made straight for "Uncle" Giles's shop. He found the miser in a state of clamminess.

"Come in, lad," he whined. "Come right in! Here, hae a cigar. Tak' twa!" And after this unprecedented fit of generosity, Old Scryme started to lock up the shop.

"Stop that, you old shrimp!" cried Smuggle-erie. "If you can't keep your head straight, lock up your conscience, but leave that door alone. Come here! Sit down! Hand me an apple! Give me a light! Hold it!" Puff—Puff—Puff. "There, now! Be a good little nunky, and do as you're told."

"Aye, aye, lad," the miser made haste to answer. "But losh! it's the sair fright I've had this day. Guid help us! What does it a' mean? Here's the Thistle Down come back, an' a' sorts o' didoes kicking up, an' runnin' the gantlet in broad day, an' the cap'n carried ashore on a stretcher, an' a revenue off'cer spoutin' Latin, an' the laird skedaddled to Edinbro'. What's it a' aboot?"

"And so the laird's skedaddled, eh?" said Smuggle-erie. "Well, he's a good riddance. There never was a bigger coward, unless it's yourself. And how's nunky feeling, hey?" He poked Giles in the ribs. Giles gave a scream of hysterical laughter, and then sat down in a quaking heap.

"For Heaven's sake, haud off!" he gurgled. "Ye'll be the death o' me."

"I always said so—swore so—and meant so!" was the cool assertion.

"Aye, aye!" with a silly giggle. "Ye will hae yer joke. But tell a man, Smuggle-erie. Hae another cigar? Tak' the box. Ye ken where they come frae—hey, lad? Noo, tell's aboot it."

"Well," said Smuggle-erie, drawing a long, luxurious, deliberate whiff from his cigar. "As they say in the kirk when somebody's taken bad, owing to a sudden indisposition on the part of Captain Grant, and thinking it would be better to bring him home alive than in a barrel—I mean, a coffin—I put back into Morag."

"Aye, lad," said Giles, overlooking the peculiar slip; "but—but the—whusky, lad?"

"And in order to save ourselves—that is, *you* for instance," continued Smuggle-erie airily, "I made a virtue of a necessity, as the dominie would say——"

"Never mind the dominie!" Old Scryme protested.

"And threw every keg of it overboard!"

"Eh?" gasped Giles, relief dawning upon his face.

"Weel done, lad—weel done! But what a waste—what a waste!" he added mournfully.

Smuggle-erie took the cigar from his mouth, stared at nunky with big solemn eyes, and finally blurted out:

"My, but you're thrifty!"

"Aye, aye, lad! But I dare say it was a' for the best—a' for the best."

"Imphm!" hummed Smuggle-erie. "A' for the best—maybe."

"But what about yon barrel?" whispered Old Scryme. "What devil's prank was yon?"

"Oh, that!" said Smuggle-erie carelessly. "As you say, nunky, I will hae my joke, an' that was my bit joke on the lufftenant, just to show the coastguard that they are no match for the lads o' Morag, even in broad daylight."

"Aye, aye!" chuckled Giles. "Ye will hae yer joke. But ye're awfu' reckless—fearfu' reckless. But where's the barrel, Smuggle-erie?"

"Ah!" said Smuggle-erie knowingly, and wagging his finger in nunky's face. "That's just it! Where's the barrel? They say they saw a barrel. Well, where's the barrel? Barrel, barrel, who's got the barrel? I can see the lord advocate laughing."

"Wheesht, man!" cried Giles in agony. "Dinna talk aboot sic a person. But where's the barrel, lad? Ye can surely tell nunky."

" Barrel! " roared Smuggle-erie, suddenly losing his temper. " Is everybody daft? What barrel? I never saw a barrel! It wasna a barrel ye saw—*it was a ghost!* Boo! "

Smuggle-erie said it in such a way that Giles's weak heart nearly ceased to beat for all time. He leaned heavily against the counter and gasped for breath:

" Losh, Smuggle-erie, ye're a clever lad, but awfu' reckless—unco reckless! "

" Well, don't let me hear any more about that barrel! " Smuggle-erie shouted, shaking his fist in Old Scryme's face. " *Where's Horneycraft?* "

" I—I dunno! " whined Old Scryme.

" Neither do I," chuckled Smuggle-erie, his eyes twinkling.

With that he walked out, puffing the contraband cigar, and quite regardless of the fact that his guardian was lying across the counter, fighting for the breath of life, and blue with agony.

Smuggle-erie walked to the coast-guard station on the barren rocks at the north end of the village. In the parlor he was received by the dominie and Jack Cookson, the former grave and disapproving, the latter tempestuous and purple.

" Well, sir! " thundered Jack Cookson. " I suppose you've come to turn king's evidence, like an honest man."

"Exactly what I've come for," said Smuggle-erie coolly.

"Then, by thunder! it's just what I'd expect of such a rapscallious rogue."

"Is the lieutenant well enough to take down what I have to say?" asked Smuggle-erie of the dominie.

"Tut, tut! What's all this nonsense?" the dominie stammered, completely taken aback. "King's evidence! King's evidence?"

"That's what I said."

"Tut, tut! My dear young man—I—I—the fact is,—I think—indeed, I may say, from a professional standpoint, that I disapprove of the entire proceedings. Go away—and—and consider that what you have said is under the seal of professional confidence. I—Bless my soul, I never heard the like! No, young man. The lieutenant is too ill to hear you, or even to understand you if he heard. I would advise you to come to-morrow and—and be a little more discreet in speaking in the presence of one who is not only a medico, but a bailie in the land."

With that he turned his back on both Smuggle-erie and the coast-guard and vanished into the sick-room.

"What!" snorted Cookson. "Is it possible he's a smuggler, too? Is it possible *I* have nursed a wampire at my heart? *By—thunder!*"

"Not a bit," said Smuggle-erie with a laugh.

[207]

"He's no smuggler—just a good old soul. He's been up at the cottage, hasn't he?"

"That he has."

"I thought so. 'Morning, Coast-guard."

And Smuggle-erie went away, looking very grave. He understood the dominie's reprimand; but, then, the dominie, he reflected, didn't know all that he knew.

Smuggle-erie, himself, went to the cottage with the flagstaff. Mrs. Martin met him at the door with a face that would have shamed saltpeter.

"How's the skipper?" he asked earnestly.

"None of your business, ye heathen malefactor!" she sniffed.

"I want to see him."

"Ye can't!"

"Well, I must see Grizel."

"Ye sha'n't!"

"Very well," said Smuggle-erie sadly. Presently he brightened up. "Perhaps it's just as well. But if the skipper wakes up and looks to be uneasy about anything, tell him to leave it all to Smuggle-erie!"

Later, he went aboard the Thistle Down. Most of the crew had returned, in order to evade questioning; and principally because they were afraid to remain ashore. Smuggle-erie avoided the score of questioning eyes that sought his. He went straight forward to the men's quarters, where the Red Mole and his son had been imprisoned in a dark cubby-hole. He lighted a lantern and stepped inside. The two men were sitting on the floor, with their hands tied behind them.

" Listen to me," said Smuggle-erie. " We are eager to save our necks. The game's up for all of us. If you want to save your necks—and you're worse off than we are, by a long sight—you'd better do as I tell you. The barrel's ashore. Where it is, nobody kens but them that ought to ken. It's going to be produced to-morrow. And you two are going to be there —*if you're good*. What are you going to do when the coast-guard opens that barrel? "

Archibald did not answer, but the Red Mole looked up and said with a pitiful moan:

" Anything—anything ye say ! "

" Well, you'll turn king's evidence, and repeat just what you said beyond Ailsa Craig. Is that clear enough, or do you want to stay in there till the rats nibble ye? "

" Na, na ! I'll tell ! I'll tell ! I canna do more ! " cried the Red Mole.

" Or less. All right." And Smuggle-erie closed the door, locked it, blew out the lamp, and went aft to the cook's galley.

" Pipe up, Grogblossom ! " said he.

Grogblossom, very pale and very sober, produced his tin whistle and played a bar or two of " Pease

[209]

Brose." The men mustered in a group by the galley door. Smuggle-erie cleared his throat and spoke quietly to them.

" See here, m'lads," he said. " We're in as ugly a hole as we could well be in. You've been wondering why I put back into Morag, especially with that thing aboard. Lads, the game was up. The revenue was getting too much for us; and, as you know, this was to have been the last risk.

" We would ha' won, maybe, and that would ha' been the end of it; but smuggling's one crime—if it is a crime—and murder's another. Even if we had been caught smuggling, it wouldn't have meant dangling by the neck on the gallows; but this thing does, if we don't clear ourselves.

" A revenue officer was killed and found on this ship, whose master and crew were wanted for smuggling. Give a dog a bad name, and you might as well give him poison at once." His voice suddenly dropped to a whisper almost, and his words came through his teeth. " You know who killed Horneycraft. They—I mean he, mainly—would have shoveled his dirt on us, and if he doesn't try to shovel his crime on us, it'll be because Smuggle-erie isn't smart enough to beat him. To-morrow this murder is going to come out, and Smuggle-erie's going to let it out. I'm going to let it out, lads, in such a way that the stink of it will make our little failings seem like the rustle of angels' wings in comparison. You understand me? "

The men grunted a doubtful kind of approval.

" You don't ! " said Smuggle-erie tersely. " Well, you don't need to. I'll carry it through myself. But understand this : the bigger fuss you make, the harder you drive at Giles Scrymegeour and the Red Mole, the thicker you lay it on about the poor old skipper and the thing in the barrel, and the praying and so forth, the more you'll make people forget that the beginning of this was smugglery. This is murder— *murder*—you understand—the rankest kind of cold-blooded murder, and the man that did it was the man who was capable of thumbscrewing every man in his employ. If there's any talk of smugglery, ram it home *with the murder*, and see if you don't all come out with angels' wings sprouting out of your shoulder-blades. That's all ! "

Every man remained aboard the schooner that night, by Smuggle-erie's order. But shortly after midnight, when Morag was as quiet as a churchyard, he and the carpenter, Black, rowed ashore and quietly beached their boat. Then they went to the lodge. They entered the cave, where the tide was low, and the starlight shone dimly at the sea-end.

Smuggle-erie lit a lantern, which he had brought along, and gave it to Black, who also carried a coil of rope. Presently the two men stripped naked, and Smuggle-erie waded out into the low-tide waters at the mouth of the tunnel.

At the very outside the water did not rise above his waist. He reached his hand down before him, and presently he called back in a whisper:

" All right, lad. Leave the lamp and bring the rope. It's here! "

Next morning, Giles Scrymegeour, on opening his shop after a night of bad dreams, found a barrel reposing at his front door.

CHAPTER XVIII

A SENSATION IN MORAG

GILES SCRYMEGEOUR looked long and stupidly at the barrel. What kind of joke was this? It must be said that at the precise moment Giles was quite innocent of the contents of the half-puncheon. Indeed, it was some minutes before it even occurred to his dazed mind that this might be the barrel that everybody was gossiping about.

Then, slowly, into his eyes there dawned a look of horror and dread. The worm had turned! That was his first thought. Heather Bloom had caused this compromising thing to be placed at his door. The fact that Heather Bloom would not have dared, or cared, to do such an unprofitable thing, never occurred to him. As a matter of fact, the miser was striving in his mind to explain the presence of the barrel with something other than the truth, which was knocking and whispering at the door of his craven heart.

It would not down. His conscience would not allow that there was only whisky in the puncheon, or that if there was whisky, there was nothing else. The barrel was familiar. He had seen it at Cothouse; but, then, there were hundreds—thousands—millions of barrels in the world like it. But it would not down.

True, Scrymegeour had not known just how the Red Mole would get rid of the—the Thing. He hated to give it a name, even in his thought. But he suddenly remembered two things which Smuggle-erie had said—that about bringing home Grant in " a barrel—that is, a coffin," and also that queer explosive question: " Where's Horneycraft? "

Yes! This was Smuggle-erie's work. The perspiration stood in big beads on Old Scryme's face, although the morning was quite fresh. But he uttered a silly laugh. Of course! Why had he not thought of it before? This was one of Smuggle-erie's jokes? Ha, ha! He *would* have his joke. A clever lad, but reckless—fearfu' reckless! But it would not down.

All at once the miser was seized with a panic of fear. The whispering and knocking at his cowardly conscience became a thundering and shrieking of certainty. He must get this barrel out of the way! Morag was awaking. There was the dominie coming from the sick-room of the coast-guard station. He could hear voices among the cottages, and smoke was rising from the chimneys. He must get this barrel out of sight—quick!

A Sensation in Morag

He laid his hot, trembling hands upon it. The cold iron rings stung him like serpents. He drew away his hands, and a pitiable wail of abject agony burst from his throat. Then came the despair of guilt. He flung open the shop door, seized the barrel, and began hurdling it inside. It was heavy. And strangely balanced! He could not feel the even weight of liquid, but his frenzied imagination seemed to hear the sullen rolling and rumbling.

Toiling thus, he was discovered by the old dominie, who had been up all night between the station and the cottage with the flagstaff.

" Ah, good-morning, my friend," said the venerable old gentleman, with a smile. " Strange, is it not— and yet not strange—that the night's despair vanishes with the freshness of a new day. Hope, like life, begins another era, one might say, and——"

The dominie stopped. Giles Scrymegeour was leering at him, with the eyes of a rat in a cage.

" I see you are busy. Is this the famous barrel that——"

" It's a lie," Scrymegeour snarled. " It's my barrel. *Mine,* I tell ye! "

" Bless my soul, I had no doubt of it—not a doubt of it! " exclaimed the dominie testily.

He would have passed on after this surly reception, but something stern and comprehending suddenly leaped into his eyes. He turned upon the miser with a certain bracing of his old, bent shoulders.

"Ha!" he ejaculated.

The dominie had been learning things in the last twenty-four hours—things that had at first astonished him, then pained him, for he was a believer in the inherent goodness of mankind, and which finally puzzled him. There was something back of all this miserable revelation about Captain John Grant. That conviction had haunted the dominie. Now he thought he saw it, and knowing Giles Scrymegeour's record, he was surprised that he had never thought of it before. Giles Scrymegeour was the thing behind the curtain, as one might say.

"It suddenly occurs to me," said he to Giles, with a certain stateliness of manner and tone, "that I have seen this barrel before."

"And what if ye have, ye auld busybody!" was the retort. "Hae ye never seen a barrel afore?"

"This one—certainly! It is the barrel which disappeared. How comes it, my friend, in your hands, when so much may hang by its appearance or non-appearance?"

"It's none o' your beez'ness!" snapped Giles.

"Be so good as to remember, Giles Scrymegeour, that you are addressing a gentleman and a king's magistrate. Can you account for this barrel?"

Old Scryme's nerve quaked before the grand old

gentleman. He suddenly burst out in a volley of protest.

"It's my barrel!" he whined. "I forgot to tak' it into the shop last night. It was unusual careless o' me."

That convinced the dominie. Giles lied, and he knew it. He had passed the miser's shop several times during the night on his way to and from the coast-guard station and the cottage with the flag-staff.

"I am afraid you equivocate," said the dominie. "I am in a position to know that that barrel was not obstructing the front of your shop before three o'clock this morning. I think that article should be placed in the hands of the revenue inspectors."

Giles was in a bad corner, and every moment the danger was increasing. People were beginning to stir in the street, and several, attracted by the un-usual sight of the dominie and Giles Scrymegeour holding talk over a rum puncheon at six o'clock in the morning, were edging up to gratify their curios-ity. Giles saw that something had to be done, es-pecially as Smuggle-erie and the bigger half of the Thistle Down crew suddenly appeared, as if by magic, and bore down upon the scene.

"Here, Thompson!" cried Giles to a passer-by, and with an assumption of diffidence. "Gie's a hand into the shop wi' this barrel."

The Vanishing Smuggler

"Oh, aye!" said the man, Thompson, coming forward. Suddenly he cried out: "Why, certes! it's the barrel, lads—Smuggle-erie's barrel! Hey! Send for the coast-guard."

"He's coming! He's coming!" was the cry. And, sure enough, Jack Cookson's telescope caught a glint of the sun, as the old coast-guard came along the strip of beach between the barren rocks and the village.

Giles looked around in a hunted way. It seemed as if there was a general conspiracy against him, which there might have been, judging by the grin on Smuggle-erie's face.

"It's the barrel! It's the barrel!" cried several, and one added: "Certes it is! I'd ken it in a thoosan', an' forbye I had a guid squint at it."

"I tell ye it's mine!" shrieked Giles. "Hey, Smuggle-erie!" he added, turning upon his grinning "nephew," as a sort of desperate resource. "Is this your barrel, or is it no?"

"Far be it from me to be a judge of such matters," replied Smuggle-erie, casting his eyes upward in a kind of pious horror. "Don't drag *me* into your troubles, nunky."

"Oh, why don't you say it at once? It's the barrel!" cried the carpenter, Black, with a broad wink.

" It's me that kens it," Grogblossom groaned audibly.

" Then, if it's yours, it's no mine! " cried the miser.
" What would I be doin' wi' yer barrel? "

" That's just it," said the dominie. " What are you doing with it? They declare it is theirs."

" Then," said Old Scryme generously, " I wash my hands o' it; an', seein' it's no mine, I'll be obliged if ye'll tak' it away frae my shop door."

" But how did he get the barrel? " cried Smuggle-erie suddenly.

" Where did you lose it? " the dominie inquired pertinently.

" I thought everybody saw for themselves," said Smuggle-erie glibly. " It fell overboard as we were rowing it ashore."

" Well! " cried the miser triumphantly; " if ye *will* poke yer nose into my affairs, and ye *will* ken—I found it on the beach this mornin', and who finds keeps—he, he!—who finds keeps! That's the law—eh, dominie—you that's a bailie in the land? "

" Not so," the dominie dissented. " Who finds does not keep until the nature of the wreck which has been washed ashore has been examined by the authority appointed for that purpose, and all efforts to determine the owner have failed. In the event of the owner being determined the said owner shall pay salvage to the finder of the wreck."

"Aye, aye, sir—beggin' your pardon, sir!" put in Grogblossom. "We're quite willin' that Mr. Scrymegeour should have the salvage on the contents."

"Then, gentlemen," concluded the dominie grandly, "the law, as applied to such cases, being stated by me, as a bailie in the land, it now becomes my duty to turn over this article of wreck to the duly appointed receiver of wrecks."

"Do what ye please wi't!" cried Giles, turning in the doorway of his shop. "It's none o' my beez'ness."

"Tut, tut!" said the dominie, with a queer flickering in his eyes. "It behooves you, as a citizen and a subject of King George and his laws, to come with me before the receiver of wrecks and state how, where, and when you came into possession of this article of wreck."

"And who may this precious receiver o' wrecks be?" Giles sneered, attempting to hide his new fear.

"Ha—hmm!" said the dominie, a little floored for a moment.

There was no regular receiver of wrecks in Morag, where the ocean's bounty had hitherto been men's perquisite.

But the dominie was not to be floored on any point of law. "The law," he stated finally, "provides that, in the event of there being no regular receiver of wrecks, the coast-guard shall be authorized to act, with full powers appertaining."

"That's so, by thunder!" cried Jack Cookson pompously, as he stepped into the circle. "I ain't strong on book-larnin', but that's as the law pro-wides—with full powers appertainin', likewise."

"Hear, hear!" And the crowd gladdened the coast-guard's heart with a cheer, which he acknowl-edged like an admiral.

In order that the whole proceedings should not lack an iota of dignity, the receiver of wrecks loudly commanded that the barrel and all witnesses be taken to the burgh hall, the institution where the kirk elders and the parochial board held their meetings. Here Jack Cookson, in all the glory of his new honor, rapped order on the moderator's table with his tele-scope and opened the court of inquiry.

The whole business smacked of the ludicrous, which must have been terribly grim to Smuggle-erie and those who knew what was in that barrel. Little did the coast-guard, or even the dominie, dream that the lives and future of many depended on what was about to happen. Smuggle-erie and his men kept in the background, a sign which Giles Scrymegeour misinterpreted. He saw fear in their backwardness, and took hope for himself. As a matter of fact, had he taken the trouble to look closer, he would have seen that which would have filled his heart with abject terror—the Red Mole and his son, surrounded by the crew of the Thistle Down.

" Gentlemen," said the coast-guard, " as receiver of wrecks for the parish and town of Morag, it is my solemn dooty to open an inquiry into the circumstances surrounding the finding of a barrel on these here shores.   Ahem!

" The barrel, as I understand from reli'ble witnesses—mainly my own eyes—was fust seen in the hands of persons whom I have every reason to suspect—*to believe—to know, by thunder!*—are smugglers ! "

This he roared out with a glare at Smuggle-erie, who returned the charge with an amiable grin.

" For reasons which we can guess, gentlemen o' the jury (without goin' further into the matter), them smuggler persons did attempt and try to smuggle the said barrel to the said shore of the said parish and town of Morag."   And the coast-guard rapped his telescope on the moderator's table, and glanced at the dominie as one who would say: " Can you beat that? "

" The barrel, as there are witnesses to prove," the receiver of wrecks went on, " disappeared somewhere ahint the Bull Rock.   Dick Scrymegeour, alias Smuggle-erie, has stated that the blame thing—that is to say, the barrel—fell overboard.   Howsomede'er that was, or is, or may be, the said barrel is next

[222]

discovered by a larned and reli'ble witness in the
possession of one Giles Scrymegeour, who fust says
it's his barrel, then it ain't his barrel. The p'int,
gentlemen o' the jury, which I am asked to detarmine
is : Whose *is* the blame barrel?

" But, fust "—here the receiver of wrecks looked
like a judge about to sentence a culprit—" while it
ain't in my c'mission as receiver of wrecks to inquire
into anything beyond the ownership o' this here
barrel, as coast-guard of his majesty the king—God
bless 'im!—there's some things here as want lookin'
into, an' it's my dooty to do it.

" Fust and foremost, then, the court orders that
that there barrel be opened, forthwith and immediate! "

Then the barrel was opened.

There are some things in life which are better left
undescribed. The scene that immediately ensued is
one of them. The recorder of this tale has a confused memory of a deathly stillness, followed by a
sudden buzzing of tongues, swelling into a roar of
horror, which as quickly died again into sepulchral
silence. There is also a memory of a white-haired
coast-guard leaning across the moderator's table, all
the pride of race and calling gone from his face,
and of a crook-backed, rat-like man chewing his
mouth like a person in a fit.

Then came a rush of feet. The crowd parted and,

through the lane thus formed, Smuggle-erie and several of his men rushed the Red Mole and the morose Archibald.

"Now!" cried Smuggle-erie, and his voice rang out clear and trumpet-like in the breathless air, "say what you said beyond Ailsa Craig, when that barrel was first opened."

Then the Red Mole spoke:

"It's a lie, sir—your lordship!" he wailed. "They want to put it on me. They beat me till I promised!" His voice suddenly arose in a defiant, desperate yell. "They done it! They done it, I tell ye! I saw them do it—on the ship—on the Thistle Down! It was him that done it!" pointing to the checkmated Smuggle-erie. "It was him and Heather Bloom that murdered him and put him in the barrel!"

Again the stillness, broken at length by a queer throaty cry from Giles Scrymegeour—the cry of a hunted animal which, in the moment of despair, sees a way to turn the tables.

"Ah!" he gurgled.

And a sudden smile lit up the face of the sphinx-like Archibald.

CHAPTER XIX

THE dominie was the first to recover. Rising in his seat, he overlooked the coast-guard's right of precedence, and addressed the people:

"My friends," he said, with great sorrow in his tones, "I have known you all since you were born. You have been to me as the children of my days, and it has been an honor to be your father in many things.

"There are two men absent from this room whom I would wish to have had present. One has fallen in the service of his king and country, and little he knows, as he lies in the coast-guard house, that his labors have borne a fruit which is bitter, but just to all. The mills of God have completed his task.

"The other is Captain John Grant, master of the Thistle Down. He, with many others here, has been charged with a terrible crime. The fact that he may, or may not, be the smuggler Heather Bloom, concerns us little in the face of the tragedy now before our eyes. That matter I leave for other judgment. What principally concerns me, and all

[225]

of us, is that murder has been done, and it becomes my painful duty to ascertain, by a preliminary investigation, at whose door this murder should be laid. I——"

"It's a lie! Somebody put it there!" came a startling cry.

"Silence!" said the dominie sternly. "Does conscience, Mr. Scrymegeour, thus make a coward of you? What know you of this poor man, Horneycraft?"

"I never saw the man before!" screamed Giles Scrymegeour.

"Which is palpably a falsehood," said the dominie calmly. "I take note of these remarks, sir." The dominie then looked toward the receiver of wrecks, who was too dumfounded to act. "The duties of the receiver of wrecks having been discharged, I shall now take my seat, with the receiver's permission, as a king's magistrate, and begin hearing in the name of his majesty."

Old Cookson stepped down like a bewildered man. The dominie went to the moderator's table, and took the vacant place.

"Is the young man known as Smuggle-erie in court? Stand up and, in the name of God, I adjure you to speak the truth!"

"Yes, sir! In the name of God and manhood, I'll tell the whole truth, and nothing but the truth!"

said Smuggle-erie, standing up by the table and raising his hand.

And he told it, beginning at the beginning, when Giles Scrymegeour fed him on bread and water, because " he said he took me out of the workhouse." He told how he had been made a smuggler, and how he had been saved by the master of the Thistle Down from being " drowned off the Bull Rock like a blind kitten," at the instigation of Giles Scrymegeour. He admitted that Captain Grant and the Thistle Down had " done a little smuggling now and then like the best of them," but he also made it clear that most of the profits had gone to Giles Scrymegeour. He admitted that they had taken the barrel containing Horneycraft's body aboard the schooner, but denied that either he or any man of the schooner (with the exception of the Red Mole and Archibald) had known that it contained anything but whisky.

" Illicit, your honor. I swore to tell the truth!"

Least of all, said Smuggle-erie, had Captain John Grant been privy to the matter. It was to have been the last trip, for Captain Grant had sworn to turn over a page and stop smuggling, for his daughter's sake. He had been forced into this last business by Giles Scrymegeour, who had threatened to tell Grizel Grant that her father was a smuggler. Of this, Smuggle-erie said, he could not speak of his own knowledge, but only by what the girl's father had told him in the presence of Giles Scrymegeour and several of the Thistle Down's men.

The dominie, at this point, whispered to one of the villagers, who promptly tiptoed out of the room.

Smuggle-erie then told of the captain's behavior aboard the Thistle Down, prior to the finding of the body. There was hardly a dry eye in court when Smuggle-erie, in a voice and manner which betrayed either great emotion or great histrionic power, described the opening of the barrel and the proposed burial, not forgetting the men with their Sunday clothes and Bibles, and the captain saying " a bit prayer." The confession of the Red Mole, which he had not overlooked, he repeated for emphasis' sake at the end of his narrative.

When Smuggle-erie had answered a few questions relative to the bringing of the barrel aboard the Thistle Down, he was allowed to sit down. He was no sooner in his seat than old Jack Cookson suddenly found his voice and jumped to his feet.

" Your honor, sir! " he cried to the dominie, the tears hanging on his cheeks, " it don't seem quite right for the coast-guard, and an old sailor that has served the king and Nelson and his country— God bless 'em all!—to stand up and defend any such rapscalliousness as smuggling——"

" One moment, coast-guard," said the dominie.

" We will leave smuggling out of the matter, except
so far as it touches upon the first question—murder!"
A whisper flew among the crew of the schooner,
and admiring eyes flashed upon Smuggle-erie.

" Aye, aye, sir! You know the law, by thunder,
and it ain't for me to gainsay you on any p'int,"
said Cookson, apparently quite relieved. " That
bein' the case, I'm freer to speak, sir. And there's
several p'ints that I can clear up, in the absence of
my adm'ral (what's sick abed), and which he told
to me.

" In the fust place!" he cried, gathering breath
like a rising tempest, " if, as this blame red-headed
man swears, Horneycraft was took aboard the
schooner, or found there and murdered without
quarter, what I want to know is—*why in thunder
did they bring him back*, when they could ha' buried
him at sea? Was that the act of murderers?"

The coast-guard glared around to see what effect
that had. The point scored heavily, to judge by
the suppressed murmur. Encouraged, Jack Cookson
continued:

" If, as this red-headed man says, they murdered
Mr. Horneycraft because he was the revenue collector
and knew too much——"

" One moment," the dominie interrupted. " He
did not say so, my friend."

" Well, he meant that, anyway!" roared Cookson.

" I'm not strong on book-larnin', but I know what I'm saying."

" Go on," said the dominie, smiling his apprecia-tion.

" If they murdered him on the night the Thistle Down sailed—and it ain't likely it was before, 'cause this here man says they done it on the ship—why didn't they put Adm'ral Ben Larkin in a barrel, too? Hey? They knocked him over the head that night, and tied 'im up. And, by thunder! here's a witness can prove every blame word of that, if she'll only talk!"

There had been a little rustle of excitement while Cookson was speaking and, at the finish of his second point, Grizel walked into the important council. She was pale, but calm, and walked straight to the moderator's table with her eyes lowered and her hands clasped before her. The dominie smiled an assuring welcome and, after a moment's whispering, seated her in a chair at his side. After the little excitement had abated, Jack Cookson resumed.

" Thirdly!" he bellowed, " I happen to know by thunder, that Mr. Horneycraft had been missing four days before the schooner sailed!"

This point also scored heavily at the moment, although those who remember the details of the great Heather Bloom case, in Edinburgh, will recall that it was thrown out, it being established conclusively that the murdered Horneycraft was seen thirty-six hours before the Thistle Down sailed.

" And fourthly," concluded Cookson, " I happen to know, and the adm'ral will bear witness to't, that on the night the Thistle Down sailed half a hundred barrels came from Cothouse Inn, which, as everybody knows, is run by this red-haired man."

" Thank you," said the dominie. " I think it should be easy to prove where the barrel came from. The evidence of the lieutenant, coupled with the evidence of the crew of the Thistle Down——"

" Why should it? " Giles Scrymegeour suddenly squeaked. " Why should it prove anything? And what have I got to do with that, anyway? The whole bang-jing o' them is conspirin' agin Baldy Currie. He says he saw them do it. Is that not enough? "

" Pardon me," said the dominie sweetly; " I had quite forgotten that you were here, Mr. Scrymegeour. I thank you for the reminder. In a matter of this kind we accuse none until all is heard. I do not even accuse you of complicity in the matter. Is there anything you wish to say? "

Giles scrambled to his feet, and his little rheumy eyes peered around the room in search of a friendly face. There was not one, but there was also none that he saw any logical reason to fear greatly.

They were smugglers, all of them, and he had

taken care to conduct his matters with a view to wriggling out in such an emergency. The smuggling part of it was not serious, to his mind. He was a merchant, he assured himself, and surely there was nothing wrong in taking a little profit when it came his way. What had he to do with the Thistle Down and its comings and goings, save to buy what was offered him and pay the price? He was no keeper of other folks' consciences. He was safe! He was safe, so long as the Red Mole and Archibald stood by him. And they dared not speak, or their own necks would stiffen in a rope.

Of course, it was a great pity that the body had not been landed in England, for then it might never have been traced back; and if it had been—why, then, it came from a smuggler ship whose captain was the notorious Heather Bloom. Thus Old Scryme could have wriggled out quite easily. And, of course, they had been great fools not to bury the body at sea. Who would have believed they would bring the body back? Yet they had brought the body back. Ah, there it was! There it was!

Giles Scrymegeour suddenly woke up, and found Smuggle-erie's eye fixed upon him. Ah! There it was! The miser dashed his hand across his face. It was wet. It surprised him, for what he had tried to brush away was the memory of Smuggle-erie's father, whom he had ruined, and the echo of Smuggle-

erie's promise that he would be the death of him
some day.

" Have you nothing to say? " he heard the dominie's voice ask. " You are merely delaying the proceedings."

Had he nothing to say? Had he said nothing?
Had he been standing there in a trance all this time?
Giles Scrymegeour tried to speak, but all he could
stammer was:

" I have nothing to say. I ken nothing at all
aboot it. It's a conspiracy, I tell ye. They owed
me money. Who is this Heather Bloom? I dinna
ken what—what——"

He sat down stupidly, and began to moisten his
lips with his tongue. Then he heard a voice—far
away and sweet. He presently recovered, and found
that it was Grizel Grant who was speaking. What
was she doing here? What did she know about the
business? What could she say? What was she
saying? Then his heart gave a great leap and he
sat staring at the pale girl, standing before him
like an avenging angel.

Grizel Grant told her story briefly and calmly.
She said that she had come there at the request of
the dominie, and with the consent of her father.
Until a few days before she had not known that her
father was a smuggler. She was sorry, of course,
to hear it, but she knew that her father was a good

man, nevertheless, because, when she had told him that she knew, he had promised to begin life over again, for her sake. That was on the night the Thistle Down sailed.

On the previous night, she said, she had been standing with Lieutenant Ben Larkin at the gate of her father's cottage. It was very late. It may have been morning. They had just come from the harvest-home, she added hurriedly. Through the open parlor window she had overheard her father and Mr. Scrymegeour in conversation. From this conversation, which Grizel repeated, it was made clear to the dominie that the miser was the mainspring of the smugglers, and had coerced Heather Bloom.

" You are positive that Lieutenant Larkin heard and understood the significance of what was said? " asked the dominie gently, while Giles Scrymegeour stared blankly at the girl.

" I—I am positive," Grizel stammered, a wave of red crossing her cheeks. " I know he understood.

" Next evening I met the lieutenant by the castle gate," Grizel bravely continued. " I was about to speak to him, when he was attacked by a number of men."

" Who were they? You must tell me that," said the dominie.

Grizel's eyes fell to the ground. It was the last strand between her and Smuggle-erie, and the heart

of the woman lingered with it. But Smuggle-erie
himself came to the rescue.

"Here, sir!" he cried. "I was the leader!
Talk up, lads! Hands up, who were there?"

"Me!" "Me, too!" "And me!" cried a dozen
voices, and as many hands went aloft.

"Tut, tut! Bless my soul! I never heard the
like!" cried the dominie, forgetting his dignity in
his admiration. "But, tell me, child. What were
you doing with the lieutenant at the castle gate?
Had he asked you to meet him, for I cannot believe
that—hmm—hmm——"

As the dominie broke off, confused, a cunning
smile appeared on Giles Scrymegeour's face, and the
smile spread into an evil grin when Grizel was unable
to answer.

"There!" cried the miser shrilly. "Heather
Bloom's lass. A conspiracy, I tell ye!"

"Don't listen to that shrimp!" cried Smuggle-
erie, jumping to his feet. "I'll tell ye what she was
doing there."

Grizel cast a swift glance at Smuggle-erie, whether
of reproach or gratitude, it would be hard to say.
Smuggle-erie replied with a flash of determination,
and spoke up. When the truth was out, he sat
down, very red in the face, and studied the toes
of his sea-boots. The dominie nodded his head ap-
provingly.

"It was a brave man who spoke that confession," he said. "I believe every word of it."

Grizel resumed her narrative.

"Afterward they carried the lieutenant to the gardener's lodge," she said. "They took me there, also. No, they did not tie me up. By and by— it must have been some hours—a cart came to the door and the men I have named began to bring in a lot of kegs, which they lowered through a hole in the floor. The Red Mole, and that other man with him, were there. I remember that distinctly, because the others had a quarrel with them."

"What was the quarrel about, Miss Grant?" asked the dominie.

"About two things. First, there was a big barrel, bigger than the rest, and Smuggle-erie asked the Red Mole what they meant by sending whisky in a barrel the size of a ship. That was the way he put it."

"Stop a minute, my dear," said the dominie shrewdly. "It pains me to have to ask you to look at this barrel. Never mind what is in it. Just look at the outside of the barrel, for that was all you could have seen. Is this the same barrel?"

"Yes," replied Grizel, bravely facing the barrel.

"Thank you, my child," said the dominie. "I think that will do now and you may go home to your father. I hope he is better."

" Thank you," she said. Then she burst out suddenly: " Oh, no, no! There is something else I must tell you."

" Indeed? " said the dominie, surprised.

" Yes, I must tell you. They quarreled about the lieutenant. When all was ready they took and carried him into the woods and left him there with me. But before that this man," and she pointed straight at the Red Mole, who cowered before the accusing finger, " wanted to put him in the boat and drown him, so that it would appear that he had met with an accident."

" It's a lie! It's a lie! " yelled the Red Mole.

" It's true! It's true! " shouted Smuggle-erie, and a score of smugglers yelled corroboration.

" Silence! " roared Cookson.

" Yes, it is true! " cried Grizel. " I would not tell a lie even to save my father. But that man said it was the best thing to do, and that it was what Old Scryme would have wanted."

The uproar that followed was terrific. The smugglers yelled. Cookson roared. The dominie stood up with his long, white hand raised in protest. Giles Scrymegeour was writhing on the floor, his eyes starting and his mouth chewing and chewing. Then, out of all the hubbub and confusion rushed a man with fiery red hair, who flung himself on his knees before the moderator's table and pleaded for mercy.

CHAPTER XX

EXODUS!

THE news that was broken to Larkin, bit by bit, almost made him believe that he was still in the land of delirium. In the first place, Horneycraft was dead, and it had been his body in the barrel which he had been chasing.

The Red Mole had confessed to the murder. He had turned evidence against himself, his son, and Giles Scrymegeour on the schooner; then he had pretended that he had done so only to save himself from the smugglers; and, finally, a chance shot from the quiver of a truthful girl had left him with the option of turning king's evidence or having the whole crime upon his own shoulders. He had turned king's evidence.

Now he was in jail. So also was his sulky son, the man who had struck the blow. So also was Giles Scrymegeour, the man who had formulated the cunning idea of shipping the body on the Thistle Down. So also was Smuggle-erie, Grogblossom, and the schooner's crew. Heather Bloom, a lion shorn of his strength, lay sick unto death in the cottage with the flagstaff, and the only man who had escaped the reckoning was the laird. Well, nobody wanted him. The laird had been only a tool.

Smuggle-erie's behavior had been an enigma to Larkin as he first pondered over it. Larkin was now master of the situation for all practical purposes, but in his own heart he suffered the humiliation of the knowledge that it was Smuggle-erie who was the victor. With his shrewd foresight, the young smuggler had seen the upshot of the murder, as it affected the smugglers, and had seized the bull by the horns in a manner that took the lieutenant's breath away.

And Grizel? Larkin sighed. She could not but compare the actions of either; and anyway, he reflected, even if Smuggle-erie had not shown himself to be the greater man of the two, Larkin had wrought enough damage in the girl's life to preclude any idea of forgiveness this side of eternity.

Aside from Larkin, the thing was a nine-days' wonder in the world, but before one of the nine had expired another sensation was mixed in the whirl of events. And it was the nature of that sensation which set all Scotland by the ears and wafted popular prejudice to the side of the smugglers at the great Edinburgh trial. All the world loves a daredevil, especially when his recklessness comes strictly within the bounds of fair fight.

The Vanishing Smuggler

When the dominie ordered that Giles Scrymegeour and his accomplices be locked up in the coast-guard station, he found himself confronted by a delicate problem. The dominie felt that it was his duty to place Smuggle-erie and his companions under temporary restraint. Heather Bloom, of course, was incapable of attempting to escape from the meshes of the law. But, unfortunately, there was no jail in Morag of sufficient dimensions to accommodate the number who were involved in the affair. And the whole crew of the Thistle Down was a force to be reckoned with.

The dominie finally offered Smuggle-erie and his men their temporary freedom on parole. Smuggle-erie, as spokesman for the crew, declined the offer. Speaking for himself, he would be permanently free at any cost if he saw a chance to wriggle out of the mess. The only bond that he would recognize was his duty to Heather Bloom.

The dominie, in despair, was compelled to borrow the burgh hall from the kirk elders, and here the smugglers spent their first night of imprisonment with song and story and dancing, much to the amusement of the Morag folk and the horror of the kirk elders. The latter worthies, in fact, threatened to revoke the permission and would have let the jail loose had it not been for the soothing influence of the dominie, who promised that arrangements would be made for the conveyance of the smugglers to Dunoon, the nearest prison town. In the meantime Jack Cookson, with six armed men, was placed as guardian of the jail.

On the following night, shortly before midnight, the door of the cottage with the flagstaff softly opened and someone stepped into the parlor. Grizel, who had been sitting up with her father, heard the footsteps and timorously went to investigate. She found someone sitting by the low fire in the open hearth.

" Smuggle-erie! " she gasped.

" It's me, Grizel," said he simply.

" But how did you get here? How did you get out o' the jail? "

" The jail? " he echoed with a laugh. " Lifted the back window and dropped out. Cookson was telling his men about Trafalgar."

" But—but the others? " she stammered. " Sure-ly——"

" All aboard the Thistle Down by this time," he said. " I'll join them after I've had my talk with you."

She stared at him for a moment, her face flushed with admiration and her bosom heaving with the excitement of her thoughts. Then the quick alarm sprang into her eyes.

" Oh, lad, lad! What have ye done? " she cried.

" Stolen the ship," he said quietly. " We'll put to sea before dawn. Then good-by, Smuggle-erie. Lass, have I done my duty? Am I as bad as ye thought? "

" No," she said, sitting down on the rug and gazing thoughtfully into the fire. " Ye've done wonders, lad. But—my poor father! It's like ye were leaving him alone."

" How is he? "

" He's awake and knowing me," she said. " The dominie says he'll get well again." She suddenly burst into tears. " Oh, Smuggle-erie, I almost wish he'd died."

" Come, lass. Cheer up! " whispered Smuggle-erie, bending over the crumpled little figure on the rug. " We've made it as safe for him as mortal men could. For myself I'd stay—ye ken I'd stay, but there's others to think o', and forbye that, lass, although we're goin' to disappear like magic, never fear but Smuggle-erie'll be nigh Edinburgh when the time comes, and ye'll find me at your shoulder if I'm needed to say a word more than I've done."

" Aye, aye," she said. There was silence for a minute. Then she said softly: " Smuggle-erie, ye forgive me? "

" Forgive ye for what? " he laughed, but with a little catch in his throat. " Forgive ye for not wantin' to marry a hereawa', thereawa', wanderin'

Willie like me? No, lass, I wouldn't marry ye if ye asked me on your bended knees. I love ye too much."

Her only answer was a sob.

" I have a notion, lass, that maybe you think you love me a wee bit, after a'," he went on earnestly. " But ye'll forget that, Grizel. As for me, I ken myself better than anybody. I'd make ye happy for a month or two, maybe, and then I'd be off again. There's only one bride for Smuggle-erie, lass. It's the sea, because she's as changefu' and fickle as himsel'."

" No, I don't believe it!" she gulped out. " I will never believe it!"

" Come, lass," he said huskily. " Ye'll surely no come courtin' me like that. Are ye as fickle as me, to be forgettin' your love so soon?" It was a moment of peril for them both, but he conquered. " Come, lass!" he said sharply. " Time's short and there's danger. Show me to your father."

She led the way in silence. She would have entered the sick-room, but he waved her back and the door closed upon the two men. What passed between them none but God and themselves know.

Grizel returned to the hearth. She knelt down and buried her face in her hands. What she felt and thought it would be indiscreet to ask. All the mysteries of a woman's heart were moving in the deep waters. In that moment Larkin's happiness was perilously near the vortex. The old sense of hero-worship which she felt in Smuggle-erie's presence lay upon her now like a twilight glamour. If he had spoken the word—who knows?

In a little while the door of the sick-room opened. She heard a voice—her father's:

" Good-by, and God be with you on the wide seas, lad. Ye've been a good friend."

Then the door closed, and he stood once more beside her.

" Good-by, lass."

" Good-by—Smuggle-erie."

He placed his hands on her shoulders and looked down into her face. She met his eyes, but hers were clouded with brimming tears and her lips quivered. From somewhere outside, faint and subtle, came a few bars of an old tune.

" That's Grogblossom," he whispered. " Something wrong." His brows knitted. " Kiss me, lass —just once for old sake's sake."

She kissed him. It was no mere propitiatory salute. It was a kiss—the one secret she ever kept from her husband.

Again the whistle sounded. Smuggle-erie opened the front door and stepped out. Grizel stood behind him, silhouetted against the light within. A gruff voice hailed through the darkness:

Exodus!

"Halt, in the king's name!"

"Go to the devil!" retorted Smuggle-erie.

Next minute he was running toward the beach, with the coast-guard panting at his heels. And as he ran he chuckled mightily to himself, for a thunderous voice was bellowing through the night:

"The jail's out, by thunder!"

Smuggle-erie cut away to the right and doubled back to his tracks. Then he paused for a moment and looked around him. The Thistle Down swung at her moorings. To his straining ears came the creaking of blocks and tackle. They were making sail. If only they would weigh anchor. How was he to warn them? Would they hear the coast-guard's voice?

Again a voice challenged him to stop in the name of King George. Smuggle-erie laughingly retorted and shot away to the left. The scene somehow stirred memories that were distant, yet close to his heart. There was a bit of a haze on the sea, and it threatened to deepen into a first wintry fog. The Gantock bell had just clanged for the first time in months. Presently the fog-horn would raise its voice in the matter and—— The spirit of the thing suddenly swept over his soul, just as it had done years before, when he ran through the night, in his bare feet, with his shoes in his half-frozen hand.

"Halt, in the name of the king!" cried a voice.

[245]

" *Smuggle-erie!* " he yelled, almost in response to an instinct.

There came a sudden report of a horse-pistol. Smuggle-erie darted on unscathed.

" Good! " he muttered. " That'll warn them."

Then the idea possessed him that he could divert attention until the schooner could up anchor and away. For himself he had ceased to think. Grizel was in his heart, and youth was in his memory. He had no desire to leave Morag. There was only one place in the world—Morag; only one girl—Grizel; only one game—" smuggle-erie." The mist deepened. The houses loomed through it like Druidic circles. He could hear the patter of feet on all sides.

" Halt, in the name of the king! "

" *Smuggle-erie!* " And he darted away in another direction with the whole guard pell-mell at his heels.

A flash of fire split the fog and the report of a firearm echoed dully in the night; the Gantock bell clanged monotonously on the mid-reef; and now the cow of the fog-horn bellowed and was answered by the calf of the fog-horn. It somehow stirred another memory, and he found himself running toward the Bull Rock. But he checked himself.

" Not that way," he muttered, and struck off to the north.

Once he heard the coast-guards shouting excitedly to one another. A pang of remorse seized his heart.

Exodus!

That would be Grogblossom! He had almost forgotten him. But it was just as well. He'd bear witness for the old skipper. He wetted his finger and held it aloft.

"No wind!" he exclaimed. "But they'll drift with the tide and no boat'll find them in this fog."

He saw a dim light ahead of him, but failed to recognize it. In order to get his bearings straight, he ran toward it. All at once the fog broke before him and a dozen figures loomed up like giants.

"Halt, in the name of the king!" came the command.

"Let the king catch me!" was the retort.

"Fire!" cried a voice.

Smuggle-erie saw the world blaze red for an instant and felt a sharp pain in his back, followed by a strange dullness all over his body. He tried to run, but his legs failed him.

"Shot!" he ejaculated. "Pity! The world—was good." He dropped on one knee, then fell forward on his face.

They carried him to the house with the light. It was the coast-guard station. They laid him on the settle, and all at once old Jack Cookson burst into tears.

"I d-done my dooty!" he blubbered. "An' see what's come upon me."

"It's all right, sir," said one of the men. "You didn't fire, sir."

"Who did?" snorted the coast-guard, blazing up in a sudden rage.

Alas! so many shots had been fired that none could plead not guilty, nor acknowledge guilt, for that matter.

"You run for the dominie, ye swab!" said Cookson to one of the men. "If that man dies, there'll be a better man than you gone."

But Smuggle-erie was wounded to the death. He suddenly opened his eyes and they could see the pain in them. His face was strangely white under the surface tan of his skin. He closed his jaws for a moment, then relaxed them and spoke as clearly as of yore, and in the same spirited tones.

"Bring the adm'ral," he said. "Hurry! He's no worse'n I am."

A few minutes later Ben Larkin came through the open door of the room, leaning heavily on the coast-guard as he walked. He reached Smuggle-erie's side and knelt down. Smuggle-erie held out his hand.

"Shake hands, mate," he said. The two gripped hands. "Whisper!" said Smuggle-erie, after a bit. Larkin bent his head and caught the words. "Be good to the lass. She's a damned sight too good for me, and you're not half good enough for her."

Exodus!

"I know it, lad," Larkin managed to gulp out, "but to have known you—to have known you——"

The pleased smile of a spoiled child crossed Smuggle-erie's face. He looked up in Ben Larkin's eyes and grinned—the old mischievous grin.

"I beat ye!" he chuckled, and turned his face to the wall.

When the dominie came Smuggle-erie was dead. When the dawn came the Thistle Down, also, had vanished.

CHAPTER XXI

" IN CONCLUSION, GENTLEMEN "

WITH the death of Smuggle-erie, it is hardly worth writing further. A light has gone out that nothing can rekindle or imitate. But it is only after the death of Smuggle-erie that the story begins, as far as public knowledge of it goes.

It is not necessary, to those who know the true facts of the case, to go into the details of the great trial in Edinburgh which ended in the condemnation of Giles Scrymegeour, the Red Mole, and his son, Archibald, and the acquittal of Captain John Grant. But a fitting farewell to the people of this tale may be taken in some opinions of my lord advocate in presenting the case to the jury.

" In considering the testimony of the coast-guard," said his lordship with a smile, " it would be wise to remember that most of it is hearsay, or biased by personal views and idiosyncrasies."

Grogblossom came in for more complimentary mention from the great man.

" The evidence of the extremely unhappy person known as Grogblossom," said the lord advocate,

" should not be undervalued. The almost painful realism of his narrative and the man's evident distress in telling of his experiences leave little room for doubt as to his truthfulness, even in extreme details.

" It is difficult for me to advise you regarding John Grant, the master of the schooner which was afterward stolen. There seems to have been no attempt made by either side to conceal the fact that he is the notorious Heather Bloom. Gentlemen," said the lord advocate pointedly, " we are not trying a case of smugglery. I would strongly impress that upon your minds. But you must also consider the character and past of the man in order to determine in what degree, if any, he was privy to this crime. The defense has told you of the man's pathetic repentance, and although it is common to hear of the convicted sinner that repenteth, in the interests of justice I would have you remember that this unhappy man's repentance was prior to the murder. If you decide in your minds that the man Grant had no knowledge of the murder, the fact that he is a notorious smuggler must not weigh with your judgment. He must be acquitted of the charge of murder."

Speaking of Giles Scrymegeour, it was apparent from the judge's remarks that the miser's pitiable condition in court had not affected his lordship in the least.

The Vanishing Smuggler

" It is because I consider the honorable jury above
suspicion, above malice, and above prejudice," said
he, " that I make free with my opinion of this person. Throughout the whole trial I have heard say-
ings and observed traits which reveal the innate virtue
in the worst of those involved. Yet of this man I
have heard nothing, observed nothing, imagined nothing which might be called a virtue. I have seen no
grain or strain of the human, save that he has a weak
heart. But what he lacks in physique the two
creatures who were his accomplices lack in brains.
The one is no less deserving of blame than the others
are deserving of pity."

Later my lord advocate lowered his tone to a softer
strain.

" In the matter of the woman," said he, " I must
warn you against the natural sentiment which the
narrative of Grizel Grant must have stirred in your
hearts, but you should consider with cool judgment that if any special motive inspired her on
behalf of the smugglers, there were other facts
which would have as readily discouraged her
from the admirable stand which she had taken.
I do not think, gentlemen, that I need be more
explicit."

On going into the details of Ben Larkin's track-
ing of the barrels to the Cothouse Inn, and the evidence which was adduced that the unfortunate Hor-

He raised his eyes to hers and held out his hand

neycraft had last been seen in the vicinity of the inn, the lord advocate said:

"The path of the honorable lieutenant has certainly been strewn with thorns. It is a matter for congratulation that he has come before us with evidence of his duty well discharged, his honor untainted, and his health practically unimpaired."

Smuggle-erie lay in the kirkyard at Morag, but so persistently had the ghost of the man haunted the great trial-room that the lord advocate could not but mention him in passing.

"It is a great pity," said he, "that neither side has been able to bring forward as a witness the man known as Smuggle-erie. The person who put about ship and sailed back into Morag with such damning evidence aboard—and that when there was a simpler course—was a man of great moral courage, despite the fact that, in most matters, he lacked morality. His statement made in the jail at Morag and under oath should be accepted by you as if he were alive and in the witness-box before you."

This charge to the jury created something of a sensation in court. The lord advocate must have seen it out of the corner of his eye, for he added with a surprising amount of spirit for one so staid and solemn:

"Personally, I should believe the word of one dead Smuggle-erie against the bonds of a dozen Scrymegeours. If it should happen, gentlemen, that your judgment should coincide with my private opinion of the merits of the case, I think the credit would be due, neither to counsel, court, nor jury, but, first, to the incontrovertible Truth, and second to the all-pervading and posthumous genius of this human anomaly, Smuggle-erie!"

It will be observed that the laird was the only one left out. As a matter of fact, when it was discovered that he had fled to Canada his connection with the case was only worthy of mention. Morag Castle is an untenanted ruin to this day, Richard Halliday never having returned to claim what was never really his own. Like the Thistle Down and those who stole the schooner, he dropped out of human ken at the moment of disappearing, never to be heard of again.

Giles Scrymegeour never came to the gibbet. Strictly speaking, he came to the foot of it, and when they picked him up he was dead of heart-failure. The Red Mole's sentence was commuted to penal servitude, in view of his confession. As for Archibald, it is still told of him that when he stood by the gallows and was asked if he had anything to say, he turned with a smile and actually said:

"No."

The charge of smugglery was never brought against Captain Grant, for reasons that were more of sentiment than of law. On the last point, however, the case was weak. With Grizel, he retired to the cottage with the flagstaff, went to kirk twice every Sunday, and spent his evenings beside the little harmonium in the parlor, or chatting with the old dominie and the heroic coast-guard.

After the disorganization of the smugglers, Lieutenant Ben Larkin accepted service in the Mediterranean. The last days in Morag had convinced him that Grizel's love was all buried with Smuggle-erie. During the trial he had seen her constantly and with greater regret for his own love. They had never spoken, and when their eyes met over the heads in court, as they sometimes did, she quickly averted hers. And in time the wide seas separated them.

It was something like an accident that brought them together again, two years later, although the word accident should be used advisedly in the matter of love. Upon his return from the Mediterranean, Ben Larkin went to Morag to pay his respects to the dominie and the old coast-guard, and also the scenes which had taken on the glamour of romance from time and distance. And it was from Jack Cookson that Ben got the first report on how the wind blew.

Later the lieutenant strolled into Morag. Spring was on the land, and something like it was reawakening in Ben's heart. The hedges were brushed with early green, and the first primroses were nestling in the mossy eaves of the rocks. He walked into the kirkyard, for there was something which should be there, if Jack Cookson had obeyed Ben Larkin's last command before he left Morag for Edinburgh.

There it was, a rude slab with rude lettering upon it. Beside it was a girl with a trowel in her hand, planting primroses. He knew who it was at once, and the time and the place sent his heart surging into his throat. She looked up as he approached, and he noticed with wonder a sudden springing of tears to her eyes. Hardly knowing what he was doing, he stopped and looked at the stone. It was just as he had wished it to be, rough and real, terse and true:

Here Lies
SMUGGLE-ERIE
A Good Friend
A Splendid Enemy
1829

Then he raised his eyes to hers and held out his hand.

THE END

www.ingramcontent.com/pod-product-compliance
Lightning Source LLC
Chambersburg PA
CBHW020614260626
47157CB00003B/1003